3 4028 09402 1665
HARRIS COUNTY PUBLIC LIBRARY

D0065074

LYNNE RAE PERKINS

SECRET SISTERS OF THE SALTY SEA

GREENWILLOW BOOKS
An Imprint of HarperCollins*Publishers*

Secret Sisters of the Salty Sea

 Printed in the United States of America. For information address HarperCollins Children's Books, a division of HarperCollins Publishers, 195 Broadway, New York, NY 10007.

www.harpercollinschildrens.com

The text of this book is set in 12-point Plantin

Book design by Paul Zakris

Library of Congress Cataloging-in-Publication Data is available.

ISBN 978-0-06-249966-0 (hardback)

18 19 20 21 22 CG/LSCH 10 9 8 7 6 5 4 3 2 1

First Edition

Greenwillow Books

For Cathie

CONTENTS

chapter 1

GOING TO THE OCEAN

The bottom of the sky glowed deep electric blue at the far end of Boskey Street. Overhead it was still velvety black, prickled with stars. The houses under the sky, which Alix knew by heart in the daytime, were also dark. Dark like mysteries, or secrets. Friendly secrets. Everyone was asleep. The three streetlamps made pools of light on the empty pavement, with darkness all between.

Alix pulled her sweatshirt closer around her. Her bare toes wished they were wearing socks or slippers—or blankets—instead of sandals.

The porch light came on at the Chebolinskis' house on the corner. The door opened and ChipChip, the cat, stepped out silently. Leaves whispered. A breeze hushed past Alix's ears. Alix's and Jools's sandals clattered and scraped on the driveway. Jools creaked open a door of their old car. Dad muttered as he tried to jam one more thing into the trunk. Mom murmured, "Oh, for crying out loud, let me try," and Jools's car door thunked shut.

Most of the sounds of the night were being made by the Treffreys.

A window lit up across the street at Rose's house, as if to say, What's all the racket? Alix wondered who was awake over there. She sent Rose a thought message: *Here we go. I will miss you every single minute we're gone!*

Because she knew she would.

And because Rose was dog-sitting Trevor, the Treffreys' dog, while they were away, Alix sent him a thought message, too: *We love you so much! We're coming back! Don't eat Rose's shoes! Or anything else that's not food!*

She climbed into the car and thunked her own door shut. She and Jools burrowed under an unzipped sleeping bag, one from each end, like a giant caterpillar with two heads.

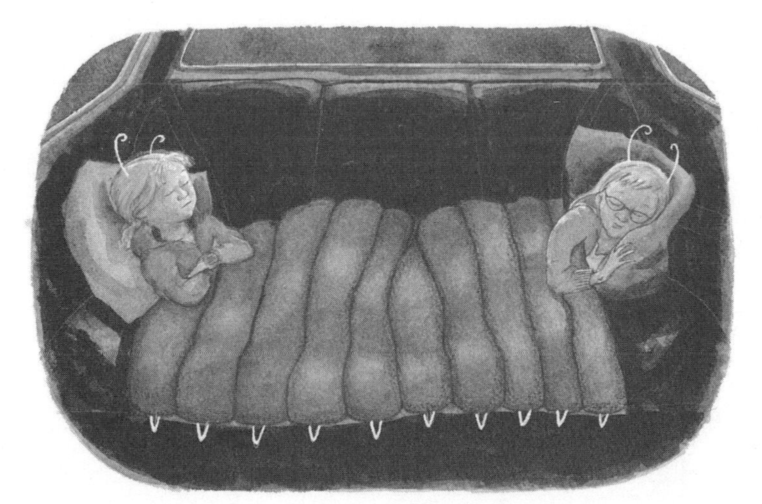

They were leaving so early because they had a long way to go. They were going to the ocean. This was Alix's and Jools's first time. Ever.

They knew just what it would be like, though. Everyone knows what beaches are like. There would be white sand and turquoise water and palm trees. They would float on their boogie boards and eat drippy fruit. They would do this for a week, then come back home and remember it forever.

This was their first vacation that wasn't visiting cousins or grandparents or family friends. They would only have each other. Alix hoped she would not drive Jools up a wall, as she sometimes did. Jools was more mature. Alix was more—Jools might say "annoying," but Alix knew there was a better word. A good word, even if she couldn't think of it right now. A really good word.

As the car began to move, she snuggled under the sleeping bag. She put her glasses in the pocket of the car door and closed her eyes. She pictured herself wearing her newer swimsuit, floating maturely on her boogie board in the turquoise water. It was a beautiful scene: so calm and peaceful. Serene. She enjoyed herself for a moment, then wondered what she could do to liven it up.

But since it was basically still nighttime, she didn't wonder too hard. She floated serenely back to sleep.

Jools kept her glasses on, but she slept, too.

So they didn't even notice how Shembleton slipped away behind them. They didn't see the edges of the clouds turn pink and gold as the sun peeped up over the horizon, making the trees and fields glow green, all rich and alive, almost magical.

Like it was a whole new world or something.

By the time they woke up, everything looked ordinary. It was a sunny day, and they were zipping along through the countryside.

So were a lot of other people. Cars and trucks, buses and motorcycles, all speeding along together. Across the median, everyone zoomed in the opposite direction. The houses and farms sprinkled off to the sides were content to stay still.

Alix and Jools changed from their pajamas to their daytime clothes. They were experts at changing tops inside their sweatshirts. The sleeves hung limp while the main parts bulged and bubbled like cats in a bag. They put their shorts on under the sleeping bag and emerged fresh and crisp.

Meanwhile, the highway sliced through hills, showing the twisting, crumpled layers of rock, like in a science diagram. Or it clung to the outsides of the hills, rising and falling in long slow curves. Or short tight curves. Sometimes it tunneled right under a mountain. When that happened, Alix and Jools stopped whatever they were doing, which was mostly nothing, and tried to hold their breath until they came out on the other side.

Sometimes Jools won, because she was older and her lungs were bigger and more experienced. Sometimes Alix won, because she was more determined. Although she missed breathing. She was so used to it. She listened to their parents talking to keep from thinking about how her lungs were about to burst.

They kept talking about someone named Mrs. Kerr: Mrs. Kerr says she has bikes we can use. Mrs. Kerr says it might rain later in the week, but mostly the weather should be very good. Mrs. Kerr says there is an excellent bakery right down the block, and we will *definitely* want to try their cinnamon rolls. Mrs. Kerr says this, Mrs. Kerr says that. Whoever Mrs. Kerr was, she had a lot to say about what Alix and Jools and Mom and Dad would be doing on their vacation.

"Who's Mrs. Kerr?" asked Alix. As she asked, the breath from her lungs escaped through her mouth. She heard Jools clapping. The car filled with sunlight and they drove out of the tunnel. Jools exhaled loudly.

"I win," she said.

Alix shrugged.

"Who's Mrs. Kerr, Mom?" she asked again. As if she had more important things to think about than holding her breath the longest.

"She owns the house we'll be staying in," said Mom. "She lives upstairs, and we'll stay on the first floor."

"Oh," said Alix. "Do we know her?"

"Not yet," said Dad.

"We're renting from her," said Mom. "We'll pay her money to stay there. Hold on a minute. I'll show you."

She rummaged through one of her bags and passed back a brochure with a photograph of a house on it. Alix and Jools leaned together to take a look.

The house was box shaped, with a flat roof. It was creamy colored, with bright blue around the windows and doors. A set of stairs went up to a porch on the second floor. There were some bushes with yellow flowers on them, and some trees or big bushes were off to one side.

"Where's the ocean?" asked Jools.

"Right across the street," said Mom.

There were also teeny-tiny pictures of the inside of the house. It seemed to have all of the usual house things: Beds. A kitchen. A couch.

Under the pictures were the words KERR'S KABANA, then an address and a phone number. The address was 4242 Oceanview Drive.

"In a way," said Jools, "it's better than a motel. Because in a house, we can pretend we really live there."

Alix had not thought about the ocean as a place where a person could actually live all the time, year-round. But she liked Jools's idea.

"Let's memorize the address," she said.

So they did. It took about one second. It was easy, because it rhymed.

"Maybe Mrs. Kerr could be our aunt," said Alix. "Who lives upstairs."

They studied the brochure again. They could not find Mrs. Kerr in any of the pictures. But at the bottom, on the back, it said, *Mrs. Lila Kerr, proprietor.*

"She can be our Aunt Lila," said Jools.

"Her husband was lost at sea," said Alix. "But she keeps hoping he'll come back."

"His name was Dorian," said Jools. "He was our favorite uncle. We hope he'll come back, too."

"Maybe he'll come back while we're there," said Alix. "I mean, we're there all the time. Because we live there. But maybe he'll come back this week."

"While we're eating dinner," said Jools.

"Spaghetti," said Alix. "Upstairs, with Aunt Lila. Because she gets so sad eating spaghetti all by herself."

"It was Uncle Dorian's favorite food," said Jools. "I feel sad eating it, too. Maybe we should just never eat spaghetti."

"And then the door bursts open!" said Alix.

"And there he is!" said Jools. "Aunt Lila faints from joy."

"I'm going to faint, too," said Alix. "I never fainted before. I want to see what it's like. Maybe we'll all faint. We'll be lying all over the floor and Uncle Dorian will be like, 'Oh, no! What happened?!' "

"I won't faint," said Mom. "I never faint."

"I might faint," said Dad. "I haven't decided yet."

"But speaking of dinner," said Mom. "How's about we stop for lunch?"

So they stopped at a service plaza.

Where a small terrible thing happened.

The service plaza was crowded. They had to wait in line for a long time to order their food. But that wasn't terrible. It was just how it was.

They also had to wait a long time to get their food. That was maybe a little bit terrible, but not very.

Then they had to eat standing up, by a counter, because all of the places to sit down were taken.

sorry
excuse me-

"I don't mind," said Dad. "We've been sitting for hours. It feels good to stand up." So that was okay, too. They huddled next to the counter with the napkins and ketchup and plastic forks. People said, "Excuse me," as they reached over and around the Treffreys for napkins and ketchup and forks.

When the Treffreys finished eating, they shuffled in their huddle through the hubbub. They shuffled past the large YOU ARE HERE map, past the coffee shop, and past the gift shop.

Behind the glass wall of the gift shop, Alix could see tidy stacks of T-shirts, coffee mugs in a pyramid, and small heaps of stuffed animals. Then the wall ended, and right beside her was a spinning rack of mini–license plates with names on them that you could put on your bike. And right there with all the other names was a license plate that said ALIX. It was red and white. ALIX.

She stopped in her tracks. She had never seen anything with her name already printed on it before. She looked away and looked back, to make sure she wasn't

seeing things. But there it was: ALIX. She touched it. She lifted it up a little. There was another ALIX behind it! She lifted that one up. Another ALIX. Three ALIXes.

Her family had shuffled on, but Alix could see the top of her dad's head not far off, just outside the exit door. She dodged and darted through the crowd toward his familiar khaki shorts. She grabbed his hand with both of hers and told him all about the license plate.

"Do you think we could get it?" she asked. "It could be my souvenir. Also, this means that other people have my same name. I've never met someone with my same exact name!"

Her dad stopped walking, and Alix looked up, hopeful. She saw a friendly face that might have been someone's dad's face, but it was not her own dad's face. She let go of the man's hand as if it were a live snake.

She whirled around, searching for her dad or her mom or Jools. All she could see were strangers. There were so many of them, all tall and strange and moving around and noisy. Where had everyone gone?

Alix was about to bolt, when she felt a hand on her shoulder from behind.

She flinched.

She froze.

"I'm right here, honey," said her mom's voice.

Alix spun around and saw her mother. She flung her arms around her. She buried her face in her mother's shirt.

"Sorry about that!" said Mom, to the man who was not Alix's dad.

"No worries," said the man.

"Are you okay?" Mom asked Alix.

Alix nodded. Her face was still buried in her mother's shirt. She turned her head sideways and said, "Don't tell Jools."

"I won't," said her mom.

"Or Dad," said Alix.

"Okay," said Mom.

"He might feel bad if he thinks I can't tell him apart from other people," said Alix. "It might hurt his feelings."

They were outside now, holding hands. People were more spread out.

"Look," said Mom, pointing. "There's your dad. You know how I know it's him? Besides that he's walking with Jools?"

"How?" said Alix. It really did look like him. But the other guy had looked like him, too.

"Because of how he walks," said Mom. "It's a little bit bouncy. As if any minute, he's going to run up the court and shoot a basket."

Alix watched her dad bounce along. Then she looked at other people walking. There were different amounts of bounciness. Who knew that was something you needed to notice?

"What if he's standing still?" she asked.

"Hmm," said her mom. "I can still tell. But it's hard to say why. Maybe you just have to shout, 'Hey,

Dad!' and see who turns around."

Alix tried it.

"Hey, Dad!" she shouted.

At least three people turned around. At least two of them were wearing khaki shorts. Only one of them, the bouncy one walking with Jools, had her dad's face. She could see that easily, even from this far away. Fronts were easier to recognize than backs. She waved.

"What's up?" he shouted back. The not-dads turned back around and kept walking.

"Nothing," called Alix. "I just wanted to say hi."

"Hi, honey," he said, waving back.

Jools made a face at her, but Alix didn't care.

In the car again, Alix studied the back of her dad's head, at least the parts of it that she could see. The headrest was in the way.

"Do you want to play cards?" asked Jools.

"Sure," said Alix.

"I learned a new game," said Jools. "I'll teach it to you."

"Okay," said Alix. "What is it?"

"Gin rummy," said Jools.

"Where did you learn to play gin rummy?" asked Mom.

"From Avery," said Jools. "She plays it all the time with her grandma."

"Where did you get that deck of cards?" asked Mom, peeping over her shoulder. Because the deck of cards was ancient. The backs of them were black, with red and yellow roses. They were beautiful, but also kind of beat-up.

"From Avery," said Jools. "Her grandma gave her some. She has about six zillion of them."

Gin rummy turned out to be a little bit harder than crazy eights, but not that much. Jools never made Alix feel dumb, and when Alix asked her a question, Jools would look at Alix's cards and explain, and then pretend she hadn't seen them. She was a good teacher. Before long, Alix didn't even have to ask anything.

They played cards for a lot longer than they would

have at home, where there were other things to do, and other people to do them with. It was, in a way, like being stuck in a spaceship. A very small spaceship speeding along the highway.

After a while, they stopped playing. Jools picked up her book, and Alix looked out the window. Sometimes she paid attention to what was out there, and other times there could have been herds of giraffes and she wouldn't have noticed. She was off in daydreams.

Actually, herds of giraffes, she would have noticed. But one giraffe could have slipped right by. Easily. Especially if it was against a tan-and-brown background.

Eventually, after many hundreds of hours, she noticed that they were on a smaller sort of highway. The kind where you had to stop at traffic lights, and stores and houses were right alongside the road. And fast-food places.

Just as Alix was starting to feel hungry, they pulled in to a Taco Hut.

While they ate their tacos at a picnic table outside the Taco Hut, Alix kicked at the dirt with her sandal.

"This dirt is almost like sand," she said.

"Yep," said Dad. "We're getting close. Very close."

"How close?" asked Jools.

"So close," said Mom. "About as far as from our house to, oh, Aunt Pat's, maybe. Maybe even closer."

"That's not that close," said Jools.

"It's pretty close, though," said Alix.

"About an hour," said Mom.

Which was still like forever, in a way. They started seeing signs for beachy places, like motels and seafood restaurants. But the towns they drove through still seemed like regular towns, with regular people doing regular things.

And then, out of nowhere, there was the ocean, and they were driving on a road that went right out over it. There was ocean on both sides of them. They were driving to an island, a big island, on a road over the ocean.

"I can't wait to get home," said Alix. "I am so homesick."

"What?" said Jools. "What are you talking about?"

"I can't wait to get home to 4242 Oceanview," said Alix. "Where we live. Underneath Aunt Lila."

"Oh," said Jools. "Right. Me, too."

They drove onto the island and into a busy jumble of shops, motels, and restaurants. Signs and lights glowed and blinked in the early evening sky. A Ferris wheel spun around and a roller coaster whipped up and down behind the buildings. The mini golf was crowded, and throngs of people strolled on the sidewalks.

"Wow," said Jools. "I didn't picture it like this."

"It looks fun," said Alix.

"This isn't the part we're going to," said Mom.

On they went, through an emptier stretch, till they came to a string of beige-and-gray three-story condos. They all had white trim. A few of them had colorful beach towels over the porch railings, probably so people could remember which condo was theirs.

Kerr's Kabana should be easy to spot here, but Alix didn't see it, even when she looked down the cross streets.

They passed the condos right up. They were passing everything up.

They passed up motels that looked like perfectly good places to stay. They passed up campgrounds full of RVs. They passed up huge old houses with curlicue woodwork painted in bright colors. Alix felt she was ready to knock on one of these doors and ask if they would adopt her. She could even be a servant.

"I'm small," she would say, "but I'm strong."

She would leave her family behind, just to get out of the car. Not really. But almost.

And then they were pulling in to a driveway and there it was: Kerr's Kabana. It looked just like the picture: a cream-colored box with blue around the windows. There were the bushes with yellow flowers, and the stairs climbing to the upstairs porch. The car stopped, and they all jumped out.

Alix ran into the front yard. The air smelled fresh and spicy. A hushed roar rose and fell behind her, and she turned around. Across the street, between two houses, was a very short road. At the end of the road there was sand, and then the whole entire ocean.

She sat down in one of the big wooden lawn chairs. Sitting down, she could only see a smidgen of the ocean. Which was the beginning of most of it, because of how the earth is round. It was weird to try to understand how water could stay in a round shape, but it did.

This thought was flitting through her mind when a woman came by on the sidewalk, pulling a wire cart full of groceries. She stopped right in front of Alix, blocking her view.

"Well, hello," she said. "And who might you be?"

She spoke with an accent, like someone from a far-off land. But, Alix supposed, maybe they *were* in a far-off land.

Black hair with bits of white frizzled out from under

the woman's sun hat. Her skin was the color of acorns but more wrinkled. Alix's own skin was smooth and the color of the wooden part of a pencil. Her own hair was the color of straw, but softer. This lady looked like someone's grandmother, and she seemed friendly. But she was a stranger, and Alix wasn't sure how much to tell her.

"I live here," she said. "All year round. Those are my parents, right over there. And my sister."

It seemed like a good idea to point out that her parents were nearby. They were busy, but they would notice if someone tried to kidnap her. Probably.

"We just came home from a trip," said Alix, to explain why they were taking suitcases from the trunk of the car.

"You don't say," said the woman. "What a coincidence. Because I live here all year round, too."

"Where is your house?" asked Alix.

"It's that one, right behind you," said the woman, pointing. Alix turned and looked, but there was only the one house behind her. She turned back. And then everything clicked into place.

"Are you Mrs. Kerr?" she asked.

"I am she," said Mrs. Kerr.

"I am Alix," said Alix. "I am also a she."

"I thought you might be," said Mrs. Kerr. "I'm pleased to meet you."

"I'm pleased to meet you, too," said Alix. She stood up and offered her hand, and Mrs. Kerr shook it.

"Jools—my sister, Julie—and I want to pretend that we live here. Would that be okay with you?" asked Alix.

"Certainly," said Mrs. Kerr. "You do live here, at the moment."

"And could you be our Aunt Lila?" asked Alix.

Mrs. Kerr considered this idea.

"How about if I just be Mrs. Kerr," she said. "The old lady who lives upstairs?"

"Okay," said Alix. "But you're not that old."

She was being polite. Mrs. Kerr looked pretty old. Mrs. Kerr chuckled.

"Maybe I will be your aunt," she said. "Let me think about it."

Besides the bedrooms and the bathroom, Kerr's Kabana was one big room, with a kitchen at one end and a living room at the other. A door in the middle opened out to a screened-in porch.

The kitchen end was aqua, with a red teakettle on the stove, and a round table with chairs, all painted red. On the tabletop, a glass jar with white and yellow flowers sat on a lacy doily.

The living room end had browns and reds and greens, with striped curtains, and old-fashioned furniture, with flowered cushions. A tall plant with big leaves stood in a metal tub in the corner.

The coffee table looked like a surfboard. Maybe it even was a surfboard. On top of it, a round basket held seashells and a square one held magazines and brochures.

"I like it," said Alix, sitting down on the sofa.

"Me, too," said Jools. "It's cozy."

She sat down on one of the chairs and looked underneath the surfboard coffee table to see if it had a fin. It did.

"I wonder if this is the kind of beach where people actually go surfing," she said.

"That would be cool," said Alix. "I would go surfing."

"Not me," said Jools. "Those giant waves are too scary."

"What if it's just little waves?" said Alix. "Itsy-bitsy gentle waves?"

"Then it's not surfing," said Jools. "It's just floating."

Their parents had moved into the kitchen, where they were opening and closing cupboards and drawers.

"Are we going to go over to the beach?" asked Alix.

"Sure," said Dad. "Just give us a few minutes to get organized here."

Alix and Jools decided to put their swimsuits on, even though they might not go swimming. Jools thought they should put shorts on, too, so they did. Then they went back out to the kitchen.

Mom and Dad were still fussing around. Alix and Jools were ready to go.

"I can't wait to see real live palm trees," said Alix.

"No palm trees here, honey," said her mom, as she moved food from a cooler into the fridge. "We're too far north."

"Oh," said Alix. "Well, at least we can watch the sun set over the ocean."

"If we hurry," said Jools. "Which we aren't."

"Actually," said her dad, who was reading a long sheet of instructions from Mrs. Kerr, "the ocean is to the east of us. So we can watch the sun rise over the ocean if we get up early enough, but it will set behind us. I mean, of course we can watch it set, but it will be over land and trees. And houses. Viv, did you remember to put the coffee in?"

"Of course I did," said Mom.

"We can see that at home," said Jools.

"What else doesn't our beach have?" asked Alix. "Sand? Water?"

Mom looked up from a straw bag she was filling.

"Hula dancers," she said. "Because we're not in Hawaii."

"I know that," said Alix.

"Hey, let's focus on what our beach *does* have," said Dad. "Sharks! Jellyfish! Octopuses!"

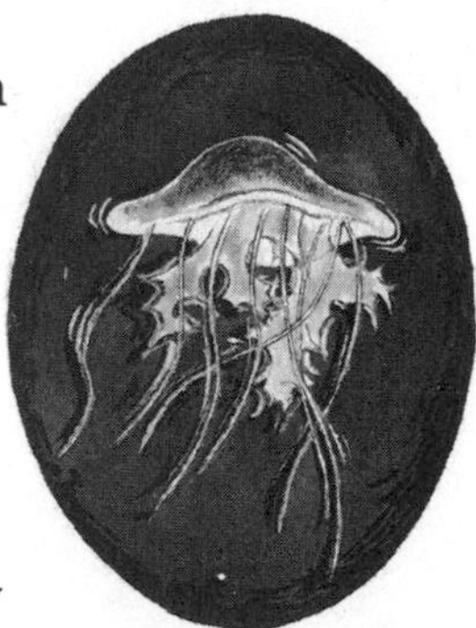

"Really?" said Jools. "Does it?"

"Cal," said Mom. "You're not helping."

"Just kidding," said Dad. "Only a few sharks. And hardly any jellyfish."

"I bet it's a beautiful beach," said Mom. "Let's go see it."

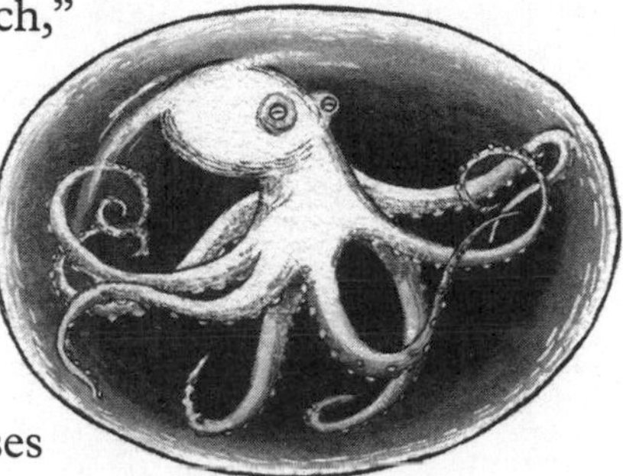

As the Treffreys crossed the street, the sun inched toward the trees and houses behind them. The short road to the beach ended in soft sand, and then there was sand to either side, and water ahead. A lot of water, wild and untamed. Not turquoise, either. More grayish green. The waves were large and startling, and they just kept coming, one after another.

A few people were in the water, though, and they didn't look scared. They laughed and shouted as the waves lifted them up and set them back down.

"Let's just put our toes in," Alix said to Jools. "At the very edge."

"Don't go in over your ankles," said Mom, who was taking an old bedspread out of the straw bag. She was always taking things out of bags. Or putting them in.

"We won't," said Jools.

She and Alix took off their shorts and stepped into the very closest, thinnest shallows. Frothy swells rushed up around their ankles and fell away again. They could feel the sand being sucked away from around their feet.

They went in just up to their calves, and then their knees. The water was cold, but not that cold. The air was warm. Alix and Jools held hands and braced themselves. They went in deeper, up to their bums, with waves rising up around their waists. Feeling braver now, they turned around to let the waves hit them from behind. It was more challenging that way, because you didn't know exactly when the waves would hit you. These were just leftover waves, anyway. The bigger ones were farther out.

Facing the beach, they could see Mom putting snacks on the bedspread. Dad had found some pieces of wood and was piling them in a heap. He looked up at them and waved both hands over his head. Alix and Jools looked at each other and laughed, then waved back, also with both hands over their heads. He shouted something at them, but they couldn't make out what he was saying over the sound of the waves. He made beckoning motions with his hands, as if to say, Hey, come help me make this cool pile of wood, but Alix and Jools didn't want to. They shook their heads no. He gestured and shouted again. Now their mom was looking and shouting, too. Mom and Dad started running toward the water.

Oh, good! thought Alix. They're coming in. And they aren't even in their bathing suits. Ha-ha. That was kind of funny.

She turned to say so to Jools and noticed that the water was up over Jools's waist. Which meant it was up over her own waist, too. When had that happened? Suddenly, her feet were no longer planted in the sand, holding her up. Instead, they were being dragged out from under her. She went horizontal. She spun sideways. She watched a curving wall of water rise over her.

Just in time, she closed her mouth, held her breath, and shut her eyes tight.

The wave swallowed her up and whomped her down and spun her around. Floating objects, maybe sea creatures, scraped and slithered over her skin. Alix knew she could hold her breath for almost a whole minute. She didn't know if that would be long enough. She couldn't tell whether she was right side up or upside down. She wasn't sure if it would be okay to open her eyes to find out. She was about to try, when strong hands grabbed her under her armpits and lifted her through the water. At least she thought they were lifting her. Yes, they were. She felt air on her face and opened her eyes, sputtering and gasping for breath. Her mom lifted Alix onto her hip as if she were only two years old.

"I'm too big," sputtered Alix. "I'll break your back!" A fact that her mother had pointed out many times.

"It's okay," said Mom. "The salt water helps hold you up." She held Alix close. Alix nestled in, wetly.

A few feet away, Dad was holding Jools. They were all still in the briny ocean, and the waves kept on coming, and Alix felt, just for a second, that she was going to cry. But her mother pushed off gently from the bottom with each wave, and they rose and fell together with the waves. When Alix and Jools didn't need to be calm anymore, they slid off their parents and onto their own feet and all four of them rose and fell together with the waves. Sometimes holding hands and sometimes not.

While no one was looking, the sun slipped all the way down. But a crisp, creamy moon shone high in the sky. There were stars, too. A million moving wavelets shimmered back. Four silvery Treffreys rose and fell with the waves in the silvery light, near the edge of the wide, wild sea. Then they waded in to shore and wrapped themselves in towels. Dad struck a match under his pile of wood. It smoked. It sizzled. It caught, and grew into a small cheery fire. Mom passed around pretzels and pieces of cheese and cups of apple juice. There was no one else on the whole beach, just the four of them.

Even though it was night, they could see their shadows. Once you got used to it, the moonlight made it almost as bright as day.

"So, will it do?" asked Mom.

"Will what do?" asked Alix.

"This beach," said Mom. "Even without palm trees and sunsets and hula dancers."

"It's the best beach I ever saw," said Alix.

"It's the only beach you ever saw," said Jools.

"That's just in real life," said Alix. "Anyway, it can still be my favorite."

"It's my favorite, too," said Jools.

"I can't wait till tomorrow," said Alix.

"Tomorrow will be fun," agreed Jools. "But I like this, too."

The flames of their small fire rose and fell, flickered, sputtered, billowed, wobbled, sparked, glowed. Always changing, always the same.

The silvery wrinkles of the sea swelled into long, dark rumples that rose up higher and thinner and curled over until they collapsed in heaps of foam that raced to the shore. By the time they got there, they were thin watery sheets. Then they slipped away. While one was finishing up and slipping back, another was crashing, another was peaking, another was just swelling up.

Alix thought she could watch the fire and the waves almost forever. But she let them fade into the background while she tried to eat around the edge of her pretzel without breaking it. While her family talked about this and that.

She sent a thought message to Rose: *It's so different than I pictured it. But it's really good.*

She tried to tell if Rose was sending any thought messages back to her. In her mind's eye, she could see Rose holding up Trevor's paw and making him wave.

Hi, Trevor, she thought back.

Probably Rose and Trevor were already asleep, though. Alix was sleepy herself. She curled up with her head on her mom's lap, her towel wrapped around her for a blanket. The fire crackled. The waves kept waving.

chapter 2

MAGNIFICENT THINGS

The next morning, a car door banged shut outside the bedroom window. Alix opened her eyes. A voice said, "Bye, Dad. See you later!" Quick footsteps ran by on the sidewalk. The car drove away.

Alix sat up and looked out the window, but there was nothing to see. She looked over at Jools, who was sitting up, reading a book. Jools shrugged her shoulders and kept reading. She was at a good part. Alix eased out of bed and headed over to where her swimsuit from last night hung over a rod on the closet door. It was still damp, so she found her other one in the drawer and put it on.

"It's gonna be a while," said Jools. "Mom and Dad are still sleeping."

"That's okay," said Alix. "I'll just be ready."

She walked out to the kitchen. She could feel little bits of sand under her bare feet. She slipped her flip-flops on, then found a bowl and poured herself some cereal.

The cereal box had a picture of an Olympic gymnast, a girl in a leotard that was not all that different from Alix's swimsuit. She decided to practice her cartwheels after she finished her cereal.

Upstairs, Nessa and Mrs. Kerr were having cereal, too. Oatmeal. Or, as Mrs. Kerr called it, "porridge." Like in "The Three Bears." Mrs. Kerr ate hers almost plain, but Nessa liked it with butter and salt and brown sugar. A lot of brown sugar. She spooned some more on while her grandma was over at the counter, filling up her cup of coffee.

Without turning around, Mrs. Kerr said, "Whoa, Tutti-Frutti. Would you like some porridge with your sugar?"

"You always catch me," said Nessa. "I can't get away with anything."

Mrs. Kerr laughed.

"Now, that," she said, "I'm not so sure about."

"Are we doing anything today?" asked Nessa. "Or is it a fend-for-myself day?"

"That depends," said her grandma. "We can go over to the beach this afternoon, but I have some paperwork to take care of. And we need to tidy up a bit. The more you help, the sooner we go. I'll wash up these dishes. Can you take the small rugs out, one at a time, and give them a shake?"

"Sure," said Nessa. She carried her bowl to the sink, then looked around. She decided to start back in the bedroom and work her way forward. There were two rugs in there. She picked one up and carried it ever so carefully, so she wouldn't dump sand on the floor, out to the porch. She held it out over the railing and let it fall open. But she didn't shake it, because a girl was down there doing cartwheels across the yard. Nessa was about to shake it, when the girl started doing her cartwheels back the other way.

"Hey," she called out. "Can you hold off a minute? I need to shake this rug."

Alix looked up.

"Sure," she said. "Hi."

"Hi," said Nessa. She shook the rug, then turned it around and shook it from the other end. She draped it over the railing, then said, "Can you do handsprings?"

Alix ran to the middle of the yard and did a handspring.

"My landings aren't very good," she said.

"You just need to arch your back a little bit more," said Nessa.

"I know," said Alix. "I'm kind of new at it."

"Me, too," said Nessa. "Your cartwheels are really good, though." She pattered down the wooden steps.

"I'm Nessa," she said.

"I'm Alix," said Alix. "Do you live up there?"

"No," said Nessa. "I stay with my grandma on days when my mom and dad both work."

"Mrs. Kerr is your grandma?" asked Alix.

"Yep," said Nessa. "Can you do a split?"

"Regular and sideways," said Alix. She slid right down into a sideways split and sat there. "Can you?"

Nessa slid down, too.

"It doesn't even hurt," she said. "Sometimes I watch TV this way."

"Me, too," said Alix. "I could do it all day."

"I could do it for a week," said Nessa.

"I could do it for a month," said Alix.

"I could do it for a year," said Nessa. "If someone brought me food. Do you ever do backbends?"

"I do them all the time," said Alix.

Immediately, they were on their feet, curving backward until their hands reached the ground.

"I can't do this all day, though," said Alix.

"Me, either," said Nessa. "The blood rushes to my head. Let's do handsprings."

And off they went, boinging back and forth across the yard.

Boing, boing, boing.

Presently, Mrs. Kerr came outside and looked down over the porch railing.

Boing, boing, boing to the left.

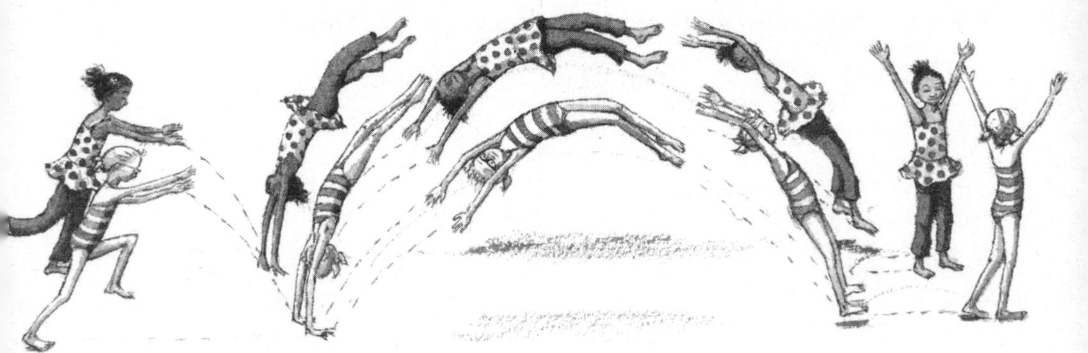

Boing, boing, boing to the right.

"You make me dizzy," she called out to them. "You're going to addle your brains. Or at least mine."

Alix and Nessa boinged to a standstill and looked up at her, then at each other.

"It's too late, Grandma," said Nessa. "I already addled it."

"Me, too," said Alix. She started to stumble around in circles, flailing her arms as if she couldn't find her balance. Nessa joined in. They bounced into each other, and kept stumbling. One of them had the idea to add some zombie-type sound effects, then they both did. Mrs. Kerr smiled, shook her head, and

turned to go back inside.

Just then, a big fat June beetle entered the yard. It was only trying to fly in a straight line, but it was a clumsy flier, and there were two large obstacles moving in unpredictable ways. It was a lot for a June beetle to sort out. If it had known any better, it might have given up and turned back. As it was, it did its best and flew forward, dodging and weaving between the lurching shapes.

And then it collided. Instinctively, it grabbed on. The thing it collided with swung wildly, one way, then the other, so the bug held on tighter.

Alix shrieked. She tried to get the bug off her arm, but she didn't want to touch it. It was as big as a robin's egg, but brown and shiny.

The bug, panicked, hung on for dear life. The tiny grabby claws at the ends of its gangly legs dug into Alix's skin just a fraction. She shrieked some more, and everyone poured out of the house to see what the heck was going on.

Mrs. Kerr was down the stairs in a flash.

"What?" she said. "What's going on? What happened?"

"It's a June bug, Grandma," said Nessa. "It chomped onto her arm."

"It's not chomping," said Mrs. Kerr. "It's just holding on. Go find me a good, thick stick."

While Nessa ran off to find the stick, Mrs. Kerr caught Alix's hand and said, "Try being still for a minute. It wants to fly away, but an airplane can't take off in an earthquake."

Alix glared at the creature on her arm. It felt strange. She hated it. She held still, but it didn't take off.

Nessa came back with a stick and gave it to her grandmother. Mrs. Kerr held it at the beetle's front end, while she tapped its back end with her finger.

"We'll give him something familiar to crawl onto," she said. "Come on, little beetle. Don't be scared."

"Come on, little beetle," Nessa chimed in.

Jools and Mom and Dad started saying it, too. Everyone was being so encouraging and kind to the stupid beetle. Alix couldn't make herself say sweet things to it. Also, it wasn't "little."

By this time, her mother was crouching beside her, her hands on Alix's shoulders.

The flustered beetle saw the stable, calm, unmoving stick and stepped onto it with one forefoot. So far, so good. It stepped onto the stick with its other forefoot. And one of its middle feet.

Mrs. Kerr held the stick quite still. The beetle clambered all the way on. It lifted its wings and flew off, in its herky-jerky way. Everyone cheered.

Then they all started talking about something completely different, as if everything was back to normal. But it wasn't.

Alix looked around to see if any other large bugs were floating through the air. She walked off a little ways, away from everyone, and rubbed her arm. She wished she were back at home with all the normal-sized bugs that she was already used to. She had not seen any beach commercials or movies where people had giant bugs stuck to their arms.

She thought-messaged Rose and Trevor: *You are so lucky to be there. I can't believe I have to stay here for a whole entire week.*

She sat down in one of the big lawn chairs and looked across to the snippet of ocean. The white lines of froth appeared and dissolved, appeared and dissolved.

"Are you okay?" asked Nessa. She sat down in the other lawn chair. "Did it hurt you? Show me where it landed. Did it leave a mark?"

Together, they looked at Alix's arm. There was a tiny mark, but it didn't actually hurt.

"I guess I was just surprised," Alix said.

Nessa nodded.

"I would be, too," she said. "Hey, my grandma and I are probably going to the beach this afternoon. Are you going?"

"Uh-huh," said Alix. "Pretty soon, I think."

"Oh, good," said Nessa. "I have to go help my grandma now, but I'll see you later."

"Okay," said Alix. "See you later!"

She sat there for another minute or two. Then she stood up and went back to the house. It took two cartwheels.

The beach in the daytime was alive with people. Everyone had chairs set up under beach umbrellas, with picnics set out on little tables or cooler tops. It looked like they were all playing house.

The lifeguards had an almost-real pretend house, up on stilts with low walls and a roof. There was even a number painted on it, like an address number on a house: 42. Their big lifeguard rowboat waited nearby.

42 Oceanview, Alix said to herself. Only this one really does have an ocean view.

The Treffreys trundled their loads over the soft, hot sand. When they found an open spot, they started setting up their own pretend living room.

They all watched in admiration as Dad wrestled the umbrella pole into the sand, deep enough so the umbrella wouldn't tip over. Then they each took a corner of the bedspread, to unfold it and straighten it out. Alix and Jools knelt on their corners to keep it from blowing away, while their parents arranged the furniture: two low folding chairs, a cooler, and the giant straw bag full of towels, buckets and shovels, and who knew what else.

When it was all set up, Alix and Jools carried their boogie boards down to the water. They grabbed on in the shallower part, where it was easy. Mom and Dad towed them out to where the waves were breaking, turned them around, and let go. They shot toward the shore.

Whoosh!

It was the best thing in the world.

Maybe even better than that.

Mostly, they rode on their bellies. They tried to ride sitting up, with their legs down in the water, like riding horses. Sea horses. But that was tricky.

Over and over and over, Mom and Dad towed them out, turned them around, then let go. The water whooshed them back to shore. The hot sun above, the cold water beneath: it was a feeling you could never get tired of.

But you could get a little bit hungry. Then really hungry. You might (or might not) even begin to feel faint. If you had ever fainted before, you would recognize the feeling.

So they made their way to shore and looked for their umbrella.

But it wasn't there.

Around and around they walked. Where was their blanket? Where were their chairs? Where was all their stuff?

It was nowhere to be found.

"Maybe it all blew away," said Jools.

"It's not *that* windy," said Dad.

Alix and Jools weren't wearing their glasses, so their seeing wasn't as sharp as it might have been. Still, they looked. They just looked mostly at things that were closer.

"Maybe someone else moved in," said Alix. She started looking at blankets and chairs that were underneath people. Nothing looked familiar.

"Do you think someone took it all?" asked Jools.

"Nobody would do that," said Mom. "But where the heck is it?"

"Does anybody remember any landmarks?" said Dad. "How about up behind us, past the beach? Any unusual houses or hotels? I should have looked up there and made a mental note. It's like losing your car in the parking lot."

Jools thought of something.

"The lifeguard thingie," she said. "We were on the other side of it."

45

"Oh!" said Mom. "You're right. Good job, Jools!"

"We must have drifted a little bit," said Dad. "I didn't even notice."

So they picked their way among towels and chairs and blankets and umbrellas. They passed by the lifeguard stand with its big painted 45 and ventured into the next maze of towels and chairs and blankets and umbrellas. All four of them looked for their own towels and chairs and blanket, their own peach-and-white-and-turquoise umbrella.

"Now it feels like we went too far," said Jools. "I don't think it was this far."

"Maybe someone did take our stuff," said Mom.

"Something's not right," said Dad. "See that pink-and-white hotel that looks like a big birthday cake? I wasn't paying that much attention, but I think I would have noticed that."

Then Alix remembered something.

"42 Oceanview," she said. "It's a different lifeguard house."

"What?" said her dad.

"The number on the lifeguard house," she said. "This one says 45. When we came this morning, it said 42."

"Really?" said her mom. "Are you sure?"

"I'm positive," said Alix. "It rhymed. I memorized it."

"I wonder which way they go," said Dad. "And if they're in order."

"We could ask," said Jools.

"What a brilliant idea!" said Dad. "What brilliant children!"

So they asked. The lifeguards in the number 45 house said people drifted all the time.

The one with the ponytail leaned forward and pushed his sunglasses up on top of his head, so they could see his eyes. He glanced out to sea to make sure everyone was okay, then he said, "It's the longshore current. It's strong today. Still, you must have been having a good time, to drift so far without noticing."

"We were," said Alix.

The other lifeguard, who was eating a sub sandwich on a golden-brown roll with lettuce and cheese and who-knows-what-else squeezing out on all sides, stopped chewing long enough to say, "Excellent!" Then he took a slug from an icy-cold-looking can of Sprite.

The first one said, "Well, keep having fun, but look up now and then to see where you are."

"Will do," said Dad.

The Treffreys trotted on. By now, they were super-hungry. Everyone they passed seemed to be eating: cheese puffs, ice-cream sandwiches, and corn dogs. Tortilla chips and hummus. People slurped from cans and bottles.

In amongst all the happily eating-and-drinking people, they passed the lifeguard stands: 44, 43, 42.

And then there it all was: their peach-and-turquoise-and-white umbrella, their friendly yellow bedspread, their giant bag, their beach chairs, and their cooler with sandwiches and pop. It was all right where they had left it. It was just a little pile of stuff, but it was their own little pile of stuff. It looked like home.

There is nothing like fresh air and oceans and sunlight and sandwiches to make people drowsy. Nessa wanted to wake them up, but Mrs. Kerr said to let them be.

"They won't sleep all day," she said.

Nessa kept peeking over at them to see. She tried to wake Alix up with a laser stare. It didn't work. She cleared her throat a few times. Loudly. Then she had to cough, to get things back in order in there.

"Nessa," said Mrs. Kerr.

"I can't help it," said Nessa. "I had a tickle. I think I'm all done, though."

She played around with the sand next to her beach chair. She smoothed it out, drew lines in it, smoothed it out again. She pulled out all the bits of straw and set them back in, in a neat row, like a fence. She lined some pebbles up inside the fence, according to size. Then she decided that they looked a little bit like sheep. They were the white, rounded kind of pebbles that glow if you hold them up to the light. She distributed them around the flat space, as sheep might be in a field. Some huddled together, some were off on their own. You had to pretend that the sand was grass. Or that the sheep were out in the desert.

She picked up one of the sheep pebbles and brushed the grains of sand off. She glanced over at her grandma. Mrs. Kerr was reading a magazine and sipping iced tea from her travel mug.

Looking straight ahead, Nessa let her hand drop to her side. She gave the sheep pebble a fling to the right, toward Alix's curled-up legs. She didn't turn her head to see if the pebble had found its mark, but she let her eyes glance that way.

Alix was already rising out of her deep snooze into the floaty, dreamy part when something flicked her knee. She reached down and felt it. She opened her eyes and saw, not far off, a girl in a beach chair, staring straight ahead. Without looking, the girl picked up a pebble from the sand.

"Hey," said Alix. "Nessa!"

"Hey," said Nessa, turning in her chair. "I thought you'd never wake up."

"Hi, Mrs. Kerr," said Alix, who was now up on her knees.

"Hi, dear," said Mrs. Kerr.

The other Treffreys began to stir.

"I brought buckets," said Nessa. "And shovels. Do you want to go make a castle?"

"We have buckets and shovels, too," said Alix. "We can make a really huge castle." She turned to Jools.

"Are you awake?" she asked.

Jools nodded.

"Let me smear some more sunblock on you two," said Mom.

She slathered away at them, and then they were off, down to where the sand had the ideal wetness for being packed into a bucket and holding its shape when you eased it out, carefully, upside down.

Alix wanted the castle to be large. A sandcastle that astronauts could see from space. Well, maybe not that big, but big. She built a generous raised area, a high central plateau. Then she turned herself into a bucket shape–making machine. They had a few different sizes of buckets, so they could make towers. Wedding-cake towers. Turrets. Alix turreted the perimeter of the bumpy plateau where the people would live. She gave them some buildings in there. Nessa gave them meandering pathways made of bits of shells.

Jools was all about precision. She was in no hurry. If her shape came out cracked, or with a crumbly corner, she flattened it and made a new one. She paid attention to what amount of sand wetness made for the crispest, most solid shape. She lined up her shapes, all made with one bucket, for uniformity, outside the moat Nessa was digging.

They made a good team. The castle was huge and it was precise (in parts) and it was magnificent. Alix and Jools and Nessa stepped away from their creation to admire it.

"I think it's pretty good!" said Jools.

"I think it's great!" said Nessa. "Too bad it will get washed away."

"It will?" said Alix.

"Well, look at the sand where we're standing," said Nessa. "High tide comes all the way up here."

"Oh," said Alix. "When does that happen?"

Nessa shrugged.

"In a couple of hours, probably," she said.

"Wow," said Jools. "Let's sit down and look at it for a minute."

So they made themselves comfy and gazed.

"You make the best bucket shapes, Jools," said Nessa. "Your wall is awesome."

"Thanks," said Jools. "Your moat really makes it look like an actual castle."

"Thanks!" said Nessa.

Alix waited for someone to mention her spectacular towers. No one said anything. So she did.

"I like my towers," she said.

"Your towers are the best part!" said Jools.

"They look like wedding cakes," said Nessa. "Sort of. Tall, skinny wedding cakes."

"I think so, too," said Alix, pleased.

The three of them sat there and looked contentedly at their huge and magnificent and precise castle. But it wasn't like looking at a fire or waves or falling snow or sunlight through leaves that are riffling in a breeze.

Maybe there is only so long you can look at something that is just sitting still.

A movement caught their eyes, and they all turned to see a boy running on the beach in their direction. A second boy ran behind, chasing him and shouting. The first boy held something out in front of him with both hands. He looked over his shoulder at the other boy as he ran, and he laughed.

He ran right toward the sandcastle, as if he didn't even see it. How could he not see it? It was huge! Surely, when he got there, he would go around it.

But he was getting really close. He was running full-on. The thing he carried was a giant-sized potato chip bag. The second boy shouted again. The first boy laughed and looked back over his shoulder just as he reached Jools's wall of exquisite bucket shapes. His foot went right through one of them, into Nessa's water-filled moat. As he lost his balance, his hands went up into the air. Along with that big bag, which he let go of. An explosion of potato chips flew from the bag. They

hung suspended in space like fireworks, then fell like fireworks—or autumn leaves—littering the castle, the courtyard, the perimeter, the moat, and the outer wall. The boy had completely smashed through one side of the perimeter of turrets. He lay in the courtyard, a giant dropped from the sky. The imaginary villagers who had not been crushed by the monstrous creature gathered round to observe him.

"Hey!" said Nessa. "What do you think you're doing?"

The boy looked over. He looked around him and saw the turrets and paths and everything, and realized what he had done.

Some people might have shrugged and run off. But this boy didn't. He got to his feet, picked up the chip bag, and came over to where they were sitting.

"I'm really sorry," he said. "I guess I wasn't looking where I was going."

"No kidding," said Jools, coolly. She wasn't usually this harsh, but she had worked hard on those shapes.

The second boy arrived at the scene of the crime and looked it over. Then he trotted up and joined them.

"Are there any chips left in the bag?" he asked his friend.

"It's ruined," said Alix. "It's completely ruined."

She was exaggerating, but she wanted the second boy to say he was sorry, too. She couldn't believe he was only worried about whether there were any chips left.

She was about to say, Why don't you go eat one of your precious chips off of our completely ruined castle?—when a seagull fluttered down and did that very thing.

Then another seagull fluttered down, nabbed a chip, and fluttered back up.

Word spread quickly among the seabirds.

"Chips!" they called out to their friends and relatives, "Chips! Chips!"

Soon the castle wore a bobbing, churning mantle of birds.

Birds in the shape of a castle were maybe even more magnificent than the castle had been.

As the chips were gobbled up, the number of birds lessened and lessened until just a handful of birds searched among the ruins for bits of chip. Only the hint of a castle remained. The last birds flew off.

"Gone!" they complained loudly to the empty air. "Gone! All gone!"

"That is the most amazing thing I ever saw," said Alix. "Ever."

The first wavelets of the rising tide welled up over the edge of the whole mess.

"It was going to get washed away, anyway," said Jools.

"I'm glad you didn't watch where you were going," said Nessa to the first boy.

He gave the chip bag a little shake. It turned out there were still some in there. He held it out.

"I'm James," he said. "He's Robbie."

"Not Robbie," said the other boy. "Roby. Like Toby, with an *R*."

You could tell he had said this a lot of times in his life.

"Oh, right," said James. "I'm sorry. Roby.

"We only met each other today," he said. "We're staying at the same hotel."

He pointed to one of the taller hotels.

"Do you want to build another castle?" asked Roby. "We could help."

This was nice of him. It showed that he could care about something besides potato chips.

So they did.

At least, they started to.

When Roby saw Jools make her bucket shapes, he wanted to know how she made such perfect ones, and she showed him. He was very interested in the how-much-sand to how-much-water mix, and it wasn't long before he had also mastered the skillful lifting of the bucket. The two of them kept on making their perfect bucket shapes, a rambling parade of them that meandered down the beach.

Nessa showed Alix and James how to do drippy castles, which called for a gloopier sand-to-water mixture. There was an endless amount of both ingredients, so they glooped and dripped and glooped and dripped. James spotted a chip the birds had missed, and did an imitation of a seagull diving down and retrieving it with his mouth.

Then they were going to dig out a swimming pool, because of how when you dig a hole close to the ocean, it fills up with water from underneath. But a swimming pool is large. They decided to settle for a bathtub. It didn't even want to stay a bathtub, though. It kept filling in.

So what they ended up with was a giant globby blob with a small disappearing pond, not far from a long, narrow forest of bucket shapes. It wasn't exactly a castle. But they didn't exactly care.

Which was another magnificent thing.

chapter 3

A PERFECT MOMENT

Alix ran from the giant bug. Not the one from before: this was another giant bug. This one was shiny black-brown like the first one, but even bigger. It was as big as a small bird, and it wasn't accidentally bumping into her, it was chasing her on purpose. She could tell. It made a loud buzzing noise *and* it clicked. In an evil, horrible way.

She raced to the screen door and pulled on the handle, but it wouldn't open. Was it locked? She pushed in the button and yanked. The rickety door held fast. She called out for her mother. She yelled for her dad.

Where in the world was everyone? She bellowed for Jools. No one answered. No one came.

The immense insect landed on her arm. Alix tried to shake it off, but it sank its sharp pinchers deep into her skin and hung on. It hurt. She screamed.

And then she was sitting up in bed and her mom's arms were around her, holding her close. Her dad was there, too, with his arms around both of them. It was nighttime.

"You were dreaming, honeypie," he said. "What was it? Do you remember?"

"I have dreams, too," mumbled Jools, from the other bed. "But I don't wake everybody up in the middle of the night."

"Go back to sleep, Jools," said their mom. She brushed Alix's hair from her face. She kissed her forehead.

"You're okay," she said. "Everything is okay."

"It was a bug," said Alix. "A really, really big bug. Bigger than the other one. It was eating my arm."

"Shh," said her mom. "Lie back down. Think about . . . think about kittens. Furry little kittens. And puppies."

She tucked the covers in around Alix's shoulders.

"I'll stay here until you fall asleep," she said.

Alix snuggled up to her like a puppy, or a kitten.

"Can we get a kitten?" she asked.

"No," said her mother. "They grow up to be cats."

"I'm going back to bed," said her dad. "Nighty night."

An ocean breeze floated through the room, salty and wild. It carried the faint *shoosh* of the crashing waves. Bright moonlight threw leafy shadows on the bare floor. They did not have moonlight this bright at home. Alix reached a hand out of her cocoon and made a shadow in the shape of a snapping goose.

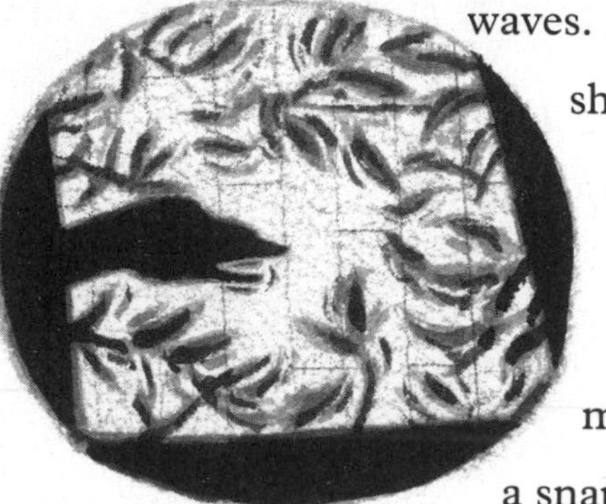

"I will treasure this moment always," she said.

Her mother laughed. She stood up and pulled the curtains together, then sat back down on the bed.

"Me, too, honeypie," she said. "Now close your eyes."

Alix closed her eyes, and the perfect moment melted softly, invisibly, into a perfect sleep.

chapter 4

THE SUPER-LONG WALK

The next day was bright and sunny, but the wind and the tide were carrying jellyfish close in to the shore. A lot of jellyfish. The lifeguards had put up a purple flag, which meant you could go in if you wanted, but watch out! Alix and Jools and Mom and Dad tried to swim, but it was too creepy, so they went for a walk.

Jools and Mom pooped out after twenty minutes or so, but Alix and Dad went the distance. They walked so far. Farther than yesterday. Way farther.

They filled the pockets of their beach jackets with shells and pebbles and bits of driftwood. They stopped

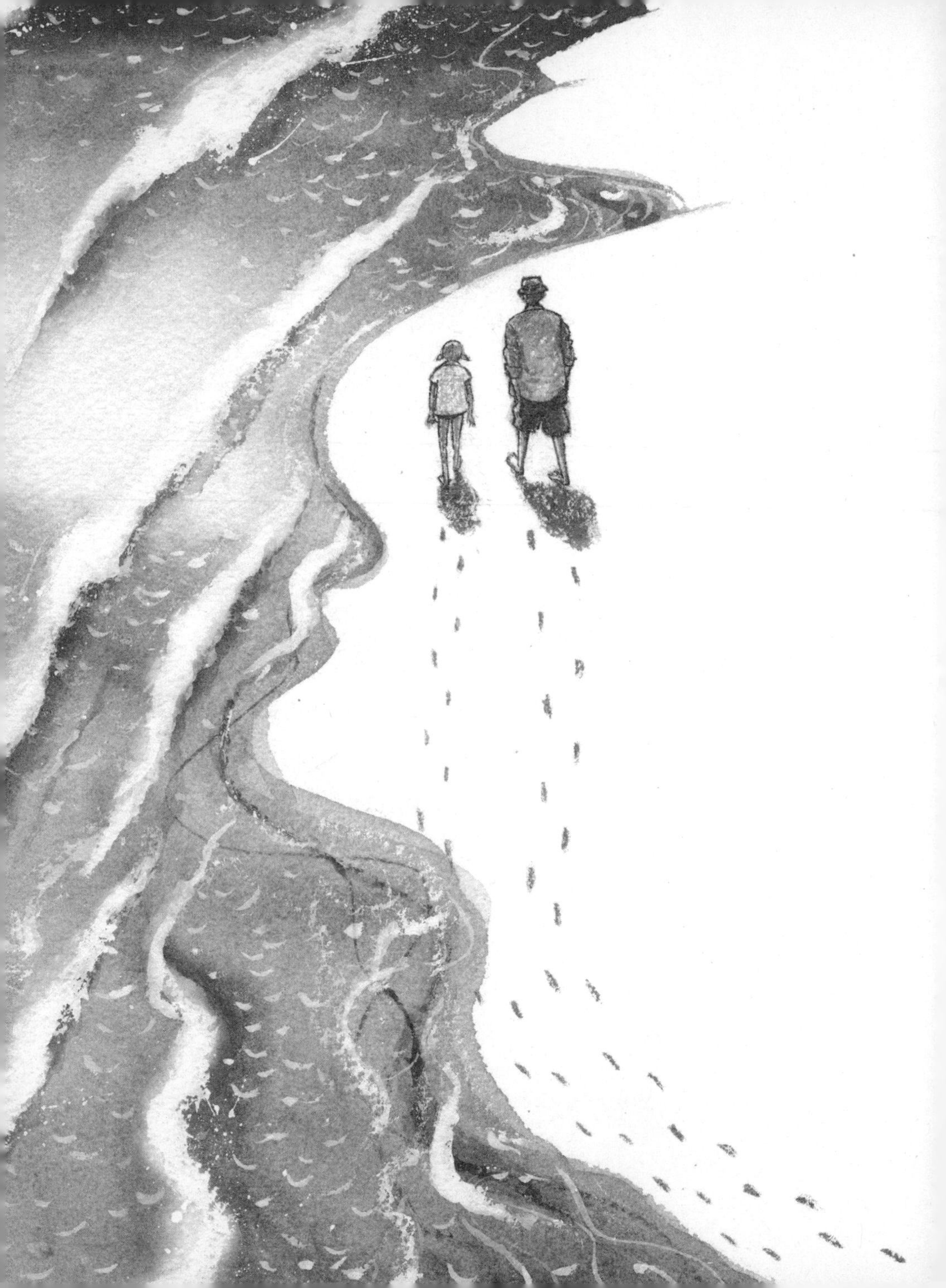

to watch tiny sand crabs in puddles and jumping bumps way far out in the ocean that might have been dolphins. They looked at huge, fancy houses right alongside the beach and wondered if famous people lived there and, if so, which ones. They came to a part of the ocean that didn't seem to have so many jellyfish and went in for a dip. It also didn't have lifeguards, but they held hands. They only went in deep enough to get wet, then came back out.

By and by, they came upon a large weird dark lump, the size of a misshapen upside-down frying pan. The shell of something. Instead of a handle, a long tail came out from under it.

Alix touched the shell. Nothing happened. She didn't touch the tail.

"Is it alive?" she asked.

"Probably," said her dad. "It's just waiting for the tide to wash it back out into the water. It's a horseshoe crab."

"It doesn't look like a horseshoe," said Alix. "Or a crab."

"I think the underneath side does," said Dad.

"Should we tip it over and see?" asked Alix.

"I don't know very much about them," said Dad. "Except that they've been around since even before the dinosaurs. Let's just leave it alone."

So they walked away.

Then they saw another one. This one was on its back. Its crabby legs were moving all around.

"I don't think it's happy," said Alix.

"I think you're right," said Dad. "Let's tip this one over."

He stood on one foot and put the toes of his other foot under one side of the poor creature. Alix could tell he was a little bit nervous. Still, he did it. He flipped it over with his toes. Then he jumped away, as if it might chase after him. But it didn't. It just sat there.

"I think it's wondering, 'Hey, what just happened?'" said Alix.

"I'm not sure it has that much brain power," said Dad. "I think it already forgot it was ever on its back."

"Maybe," said Alix. "Or maybe when it gets in the

ocean again, it will tell all its friends. It will be like, 'There I was, stuck on my back. I thought it was the end for me. And then, a miracle happened!'"

"And then," said her dad, "one of its friends will say, 'Hey, that same thing happened to my friend's cousin!'"

"It will be something they talk about," said Alix, "Like, 'Remember that time?'"

"Or maybe, 'I was abducted by aliens!'" said Dad. "'But they were friendly aliens. They saved my life!'"

"How far have we walked, do you think?" asked Alix.

"Oh, I'd say about five miles," said her dad. "More or less."

"Really?" said Alix. "Five miles? Do you think we should go back?"

"Yep," said her dad. "I think we should."

So they turned around.

"What if we get tired?" asked Alix. "Or what if we get hungry?"

"I'm hungry right now," said Dad. "Let's keep our eyes peeled for someplace to grab a bite."

"What if we don't find any?" asked Alix.

"Then we'll have to eat jellyfish," said Dad.

"Yuck," said Alix.

"No kidding," said Dad.

But before long, there was a food stand with hot dogs and pizza and nachos and lemonade. They had one of everything. All of it was delicious.

"Hunger is the best sauce," said Dad. "How are you doing? Do you think you can walk all the way back? I could call Mom to come and get us."

"No," said Alix. "I can do it. I'm fine."

And she was. She didn't complain, not even one time. Sometimes they talked, and sometimes they just walked. They walked right by the water, where the sand was firmer and it was easier.

"I bet Jools couldn't walk this far," said Alix.

"She could," said her dad. "But she might not want to."

Alix took her dad's hand. They walked without saying anything for a while. They were back to the more crowded parts now, with lifeguards. Alix was relieved, to tell the truth. Not because there were lifeguards, but because even the number 45 stand, which had seemed so far away yesterday, today felt almost like home.

She thought she saw James and Roby running around up by the hotels, but she didn't care. Not at that moment.

"Look," said her dad, pointing. "I see our umbrella."

Alix looked for it. She found it.

"I see it, too," she said.

It was the only peach-and-white-and-turquoise bump amongst a sea of many bumps of other colors.

"Why is ours such different colors?" she asked.

"It's old," said Dad. "But it makes it easy to find. Sometimes. If you're close enough."

The striped bump slowly grew bigger. They could see a shadow under it. They could see two people sitting in the shadow. Mom and Jools. Alix was glad to see them. She ran to the umbrella.

"You lazy bums!" she said. "We just walked ten miles!"

"Well, congratulations!" said Mom.

"You win," said Jools.

"What did you guys do?" asked Alix.

"We made a drippy castle," said Jools. She pointed to a fairy palace of dribbly towers, with shells for windows and pebble paths. And a moat. Feathers and pieces of straw poked up gaily from the turrets.

"Hey," said Alix. "That's a really good one."

"And we painted our toenails," said Mom. She held up her feet and wiggled her toes. Jools held up her feet and wiggled her toes, too.

"Oh," said Alix.

"And we made cupcakes," said Jools. "With sprinkles."

"You did *all* those things?" said Alix. They were all such good things. Things she liked to do. Maybe she should have pooped out, too.

"Wow," Alix said. "All we did was go for a walk."

"Hey, wait a minute!" said her dad. "That wasn't just a walk. It was *epic*! It was an expedition! It was . . . it was a *journey*."

"It was pretty far," said Alix. "Ten miles."

"More or less," said her dad. "And we saw dolphins!"

"Maybe they were dolphins," said Alix. "But maybe they weren't."

"And big, fancy houses," said her dad.

"We think that famous people might live there," said Alix. "Movie stars or something."

"We had a feast," said her dad.

"It was so delicious," said Alix. "We ate one of everything."

"We saw a prehistoric creature," said her dad. "And we have treasures. All kinds of treasures."

He knelt down on the edge of the beach blanket and began to empty his pockets. Alix did, too.

"Look at this," she said. She held up a crab shell that somehow didn't have most of the crab in it anymore.

"It looks like it should live in our castle," said Jools.

"It does!" said Alix. "And so does this!" She held up a dried-up starfish.

"Let's make rooms for them," said Jools. "They can be friends."

"They can be sisters!" said Alix.

Jools looked at the crab shell and the starfish.

"They don't look like they're related," she said.

"You can't always tell by looking," said Alix. "They might be secret sisters."

"Secret sisters of the sea," said Jools.

"Secret sisters of the salty sea," said Alix.

"Silly sisters," said their mom.

"She sells seashells by the seashore," said their dad.

A soaring seagull squawked.

The salty sea sha-boomed.

It was noisy for such a peaceful place.

And the salty sisters scooped secret spaces into the sandcastle, right up until supper. Which was spaghetti.

Maybe it was because of the very long walk that Alix fell asleep right after dinner. She didn't even remember putting on her nightgown and getting into bed, but there she was. She woke up as moonlight found an opening in the curtains and lit up the floor beside her bed. The leafy shadows wobbled. She heard Jools breathing: a soft, small sound. And the muffled crashing of the waves. "Breakers," her dad had called them. It was the middle of the night.

It felt strange to be so awake, alone, the only one. Alix wished she could snuggle up to her mother, like she had the night before. But she was too big to wake her mother up for no reason. And there was no reason. No good reason. She almost wished she could have another bad dream. She closed her eyes and thought about giant beetles and tried to feel afraid, but nothing happened.

She opened her eyes again to the silently wobbly moon shadows. She put her hand out into the light and made a goose. Then she had an idea. Before she knew it, she had let out a small shriek.

And then a medium-sized *"No!"*

And then a full-throttle, bloodcurdling wail.

Jools raised herself up on her elbows and looked at her.

"Are you going to do this every night?" she asked.

Alix was taking a big breath for the next one when she heard footsteps thumping closer. Her dad's footsteps. He stopped in the doorway when he saw her sitting up in bed.

"Are you all in one piece?" he asked.

"Where's Mom?" asked Alix.

"Oh," said her dad. "I see." He sat down on the side of her bed. Jools lay back down and pulled her pillow over her head.

"So, another bad dream?" Dad asked.

"Oh," said Alix. "Um . . . yeah. It was pretty terrible."

"What happened?" asked her dad.

Alix hadn't thought about that.

"I don't know," she said. "I don't remember, exactly.

Something scary, though. I think I was running."

She leaned in to her dad's chest. His T-shirt smelled Dad-ish. He put his arms around Alix and patted her back.

"Are you okay now?" he asked.

"Yes," she said, sitting back up.

"Good," he said. He tucked her in and kissed her on the forehead.

"Nighty night, then."

"Me, too," said Jools.

So he tucked Jools in and kissed her forehead, too. Then he shuffled out of the room, yawning.

Alix still did not feel sleepy.

"Are you awake, Jools?" she whispered.

"Kind of," mumbled Jools.

"I didn't have a bad dream," said Alix.

"What?" said Jools.

"I made it up," said Alix.

"Why?" asked Jools.

"I wanted Mom to come sit with me again," said Alix. "I felt lonely."

"Oh," said Jools. "You can always crawl in with me."

"Really?" said Alix.

"Sure," said Jools. "Come on over."

She lifted up her blanket and made room. Alix slipped through the column of moonlight and crawled in. They curled together like spoons, snug as two bugs in a rug. Not pinchy bugs. Nice bugs. The nicest bugs ever.

chapter 5

THE ICING ON THE CAKE

A low whistle tootled through the open window. Like a bird whistle, but different. Alix sat up in Jools's bed, then peeked through the curtains. Nessa was out there, just beyond the bush with the yellow flowers.

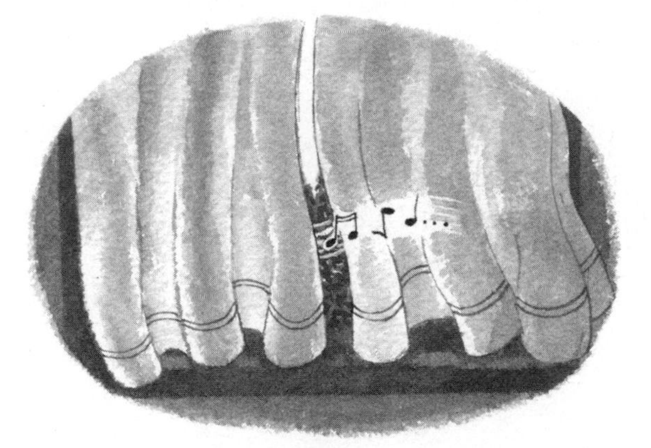

"Hi!" said Alix.

"Shh!" said Nessa. "I'm not supposed to wake you up, but do you want to go to the bakery? My grandma says we can, if it's okay with your mom and dad."

"Sure," said Alix. "I'll ask."

"Tell Jools to come, too," said Nessa.

"I'm not done sleeping," murmured Jools. "But bring me back something."

"Okay," said Alix to Jools. To Nessa, she said, "I'll meet you out front."

Her parents' room was empty. So were the kitchen and the living room, but she heard their voices. She found them in the front yard talking with Mrs. Kerr and a tall man in a striped shirt. Nessa was there, too, leaning against the tall man.

They all had cups of coffee, except for Nessa, and they stood around a pile of lumber and a tool bucket. When Alix's father saw her, he set down his coffee, pulled out his wallet, and handed her a ten-dollar bill.

"Bring us back something good," he said. "Something breakfasty."

"Wow," she said.

"You don't have to spend all of it," said her mom.

"Maybe you should get dressed," said Nessa to Alix. Alix looked down. She was still in her nightgown. She ran back inside and pulled on shorts and a T-shirt.

"Doughnuts," mumbled Jools. "Or muffins. Blueberry muffins. Or something with chocolate."

"Okay," said Alix. She put the ten-dollar bill into her pocket, slipped her feet into her sandals, and hurried back outside.

"Was that your dad?" she asked Nessa, as they walked away.

"Oops," said Nessa. "Yep. Sorry. I should have introduced you."

"That's okay," said Alix. "I figured it out. He seemed like a dad. Is he going to build something?"

"My grandma wants a trellis," said Nessa. "On the side of her house. There's a certain kind of flower she wants to grow that will climb up it, to remind her of where she grew up."

"Where did she grow up?" asked Alix.

"On St. Jerome's," said Nessa. "It's an island. It's in the Caribbean."

"For real?" said Alix. In her mind, she pictured a tiny cartoon island with one person under one palm tree. Maybe two palm trees.

"Yep," said Nessa. "For realsies."

"Did you ever go there?" asked Alix.

"Not yet," said Nessa. "But we're going to. We might go this Christmas. We have relatives there."

"I wonder what it's like to live on an island," said Alix.

"We're on an island right now," said Nessa.

"Oh," said Alix. "That's right. I kind of forgot."

They turned off Beachview Avenue and walked into a neighborhood full of big old houses. Alix had seen big old houses before. There was a streetful of them in Shembleton. She had always liked their big porches and little balconies, their rounded parts and pointy parts. She hadn't ever gone into one, but they looked as if they would have fireplaces and secret passageways.

The Shembleton houses, though, seemed plain compared to these. These houses were pea-green and lavender, turquoise and red, pumpkin and deep violet. More colors—yellows! pinks!—overflowed from flower boxes and planters. It wasn't fancy, exactly. The sidewalk was lumpy and cracked from tree roots. There were crooked fences and saggy porches. It just looked as if the houses, and everything else, were on vacation. Also, a lot of the houses had names, painted or carved on signs: Spindrift. Whitecaps. Octopus's Garden. Mostly ocean-y names. But not all. There was one called Pair-O-Dice.

"It feels so different here than where I live," said Alix.

"What's it like where you live?" asked Nessa.

Alix thought about how to describe Shembleton.

"The dirt is more brown," she said. "We have a river instead of an ocean. And the houses are smaller and more plain. Mostly bricks or painted white. At least on my street. I think it's just ordinary there. But I like it."

"My house is little and plain, too," said Nessa. "It's pink, though. With dark green around the windows."

"Does it have a name?" asked Alix.

"Nope," said Nessa. "We just call it The House. Or, Home."

"That's what we call ours, too," said Alix. "I think it would be cool to give it a name, though."

Nessa agreed.

The big-old-house neighborhood had a sort of downtown with a bank and a church and shops and restaurants. Most places weren't open yet, but everyone was getting ready. People were spraying down sidewalks and unloading cartons from trucks.

Alix and Nessa stopped to observe a large silver-and-red fish lying on a bed of ice in a window. A woman with pink hair and a white apron was decorating the ice with lemons and pieces of parsley.

They walked around a burly man who was hefting crates of oranges from a cart onto a table.

They paused as a woman in black flowy clothing rolled a set of bookshelves out through a doorway and over in front of the bookstore window. She stepped on a latch to make the wheels stop moving, then flowed back into the store.

Across the street, under a red awning, two people with aprons tied around their waists arranged tables and chairs. The scraping sounds mixed in with the fresh quiet of morning and the voices of people chattering as they did their work.

Everything seemed extra beautiful and interesting to Alix. She could imagine walking in her pink hair and flowy clothing from her pea-green house called Seaside to buy an orange and sit at the café. And then, in the afternoons, she could go to the beach with her friends. With Nessa and Jools. Maybe James and Roby, on some days. It would be a beautiful, perfect life.

A man came toward them on the sidewalk, walking three dogs on leashes. Big, white, fluffy, slobbery dogs. None of them looked like Trevor at all. Trevor was a brown, short-haired mutt. And yet, when she looked into their doggy eyes, Alix felt a sharp pang of missing him.

We would bring you, too, she thought to him. *You would love it.*

You would love it, too, Rose, she thought. *But it's just imagining. It's just a game.*

She looked back at the tables under the awning. They were each getting a vase of flowers now. She tried to think of where this might happen in Shembleton. Winky's was the only food place where you could sit outside.

"It reminds me of Paris, a little bit," she said to

Nessa. "In France. I mean, I never went there, but from pictures and movies."

Nessa considered this. She looked around.

"I never thought of that," she said. "But maybe."

"Because of the tables outside," said Alix. "With flowers."

"The bakery has them, too," said Nessa, pointing. "I think anyone can do it."

It was true. Just ahead, a handful of people sat at tables, sipping beverages and taking bites out of pastries. They sat under a blue-and-white striped awning. Every table had a jar of water with some carnations in it. It looked very French.

Until they walked between the tables and heard the people talking to one another. Then it felt pretty American.

The bakery aromas wafting through the screen door spoke a language anyone could understand.

Alix and Nessa went in.

It was like Christmas decorations for the inside

of your nose in there. And the inside of your mouth. Golden-brown Christmas decorations, all shapes and sizes, that you could eat. Some kinds had icing, some had sprinkles. Every shelf held new, freshly baked wonders.

Eventually, Alix settled on a breakfast cake with white icing and pecans all over the top of it. It cost eight ninety-five.

"It's even called a *breakfast cake*," she said. "How much more breakfasty can you get?"

"You're so lucky," said Nessa. "My grandma told me to get bread."

The breads looked almost as good as the breakfast cake, though. Some of them, the cinnamon-raisin swirl loaves, even had icing on them. Nessa considered these.

"My grandma didn't say what *kind* of bread," she said.

"That would be the perfect kind for breakfast," said Alix, encouragingly. "Raisins are really healthy."

She looked over to where a few people stood in line at the counter and said, "I guess we have to get in line. Are you ready?"

"Yep," said Nessa. "Let's go."

They took their place behind a balding gentleman in a snowy white shirt and crisp gray trousers. His shoes were black and shiny. As Alix was noticing what a snappy dresser he was, he turned around and said, "Good morning, ladies! And how are you today?"

She looked up and saw a remarkable nose. It was remarkable not only in its size, since it was perhaps the biggest one she had ever seen, but in its shape: it shot straight out from between the man's thick, silvery eyebrows, then turned sharply south between his calm, jolly eyes toward his neatly trimmed mustache. It ended roundly, like a ripe plum or a small peach, about an inch out from his lower lip.

Alix could not help looking at the nose as if it were an unfamiliar object she was trying to identify. Maybe she only looked at it for a second or two, but she knew even that was too long, and she made herself look right at his eyes.

"I'm fine," she said. "Thank you."

"I'm fine, too," said Nessa. "How are you?"

"Thank you so much for asking," said the man. "I'm pretty sure I'm fine as well. Though others might say differently."

"Can I help you, Mr. M.?" asked the girl behind the counter, and Mr. M. turned around to place his order.

Alix and Nessa looked at each other. Their eyes spoke silently of the unexpected nose. Alix put her finger to her nose, meaning, Wow! Nessa put her finger to her lips, meaning, Shh! Then they both faced forward.

A moment later, Mr. M. turned to leave. He reached into his bag and pulled out a glazed doughnut.

"Stay away from sugar," he said to Alix and Nessa. "It makes your nose get big." He took a bite of the doughnut, wiggled his silvery eyebrows up and down, and left. Alix and Nessa turned, not saying a word, to watch him go. They heard him laughing as he went out the door.

They didn't take Mr. M.'s advice, though. On the walk back, Alix reached into her bakery box and snitched a little piece of the crumbly, nutty icing.

"Watch my face," she said. She popped the icing bit into her mouth and swallowed it. "Is my nose getting bigger?"

Nessa laughed. "No," she said. "I don't think it happens right away. I think it takes, like, fifty years." She reached into her bag and pinched some icing from the top of the cinnamon bread.

"Watch mine," she said. She ate the icing and held still so Alix could observe her nose.

"No," she said. "But you're getting bald. And old."

"It's worth it," said Nessa, and she pinched another schnibble. "I wonder if my icing is the same as yours."

They decided to do a taste test. It took a lot of tastes.

"I think they're exactly the same," said Nessa.

"So do I," said Alix.

As they walked by the houses with names, Alix saw one called Rosebud, and she thought of Rose again. She had not thought about Rose every single minute. Or even very many minutes. She thought about her now, very hard, to make up for lost time. She also thought about Trevor.

I miss you both so, so much! she thought. *I can't wait to see you again!*

Which was true and not true at the same time. She knew she would be really happy to see them. But she was having a good time right where she was, with Nessa. Did that mean she was a terrible friend?

"Do you have a best friend?" she asked.

"I have two best friends," said Nessa. "Charlotte and Kiko. And I have a bunch of almost-best friends."

"I have one best friend," said Alix. "Not counting Jools and our dog, Trevor, my best friend is Rose. I guess I have almost-best friends, too. I guess Bobby and Emily are my almost-best friends."

"I know two Emilys," said Nessa. "They're both in my class at school. Actually, one is Emilia. Which I think is Spanish for Emily." She reached into her bag for a bit of icing and let it melt on her tongue.

Alix reached into her box and found an icing-covered nut.

On they went, talking and nibbling. Before they knew it, they were back at Mrs. Kerr's.

"Are you going to the beach?" asked Alix.

"No," said Nessa. "My mom and dad both have today off. I think we're going somewhere else."

"Will you be here tomorrow?" asked Alix.

"No," said Nessa. "But I'm here all day Friday. And Friday night, I'm sleeping over."

"Oh, good!" said Alix. Because she already missed Nessa. "Well, see you the day after tomorrow, then!"

"See you then!" said Nessa.

They gave each other a quick, one-armed hug, since they were still both holding bakery in their other hands. Then Nessa went up the stairs.

Alix went into the screened porch. Jools was on the porch, drawing a picture of a horse. She was copying it from a book. It was a super-excellent drawing. It looked really realistic.

"Took you long enough," she said.

"Sorry," said Alix. "It was worth it, though. Look what I got."

She lifted the lid of the white box and held it so

that Jools could look inside.

"What is it?" said Jools.

"It's a breakfast cake," said Alix. "The icing is so-o-o-o good. I tasted it." She turned the box to see if you could tell where she had pinched the bits of icing away.

"Uh-oh," she said. Because there did not seem to be much icing left at all. Just a few icing-topped peaks rose from the ravaged cakey landscape. It looked like their sandcastle after the seagulls got finished with it.

She had ruined it.

Her dad stepped onto the porch from inside the house.

"What did you bring us, pinky-winky?" he asked, cheerfully.

Alix felt her heart falling. Sugar jangled around through all the different parts of her. She could not face her so-great dad, who had given her ten dollars to go to the bakery. She set the box on the table and walked, head down, tears filling her eyes, to the bedroom. The closet door stood open. She went inside, sat

down in the corner, her face on her knees, her arms wrapped around them. She hated feeling so stupid. She sat there forever.

For the first part of forever, she had no words. Just bad feelings. At home, when she was sick or sad, Trevor would curl up next to her. It always made her feel better.

She tried to pretend he was curled up next to her now.

But when she opened her eyes, she was still alone, far from home, in a closet. She closed them again. Maybe she would just stay here until the vacation was over.

By and by, someone came into the room. The person stopped outside the closet. Alix did not look up. The person came into the closet and sat down on the floor next to her. It was her dad. Alix could just tell. She turned her head the smallest amount and peeked. There were his big hairy toes. She recognized them right away. Then the person cleared his throat. It was totally her dad.

"So," he said. "How about those Wildcats?"

The Wildcats were the baseball team they rooted for. "How about those Wildcats?" was something people said right after they said "Hi," and "How's it going?" Or when they couldn't think of anything else to say. Or if they wanted to change the subject.

The thing you said back was, "Go, Cats!" or maybe,

"Those Cats aren't too wild this year, are they?" Something like that. Sort of jokey.

Alix didn't feel jokey. She didn't say anything.

"Hey," said her dad. "We were talking to Mrs. Kerr. She told us about a place we can go to collect periwinkles."

"Periwinkles?" said Alix.

"Periwinkles," said her dad. "They're a kind of seafood. They're shellfish: like clams, only smaller. We can pick them right off the rocks at low tide and cook them for dinner. I thought we could go do that this afternoon. What do you think?"

"Seafood," said Alix. "Sea Food. Like what mermaids eat."

"Exactly!" said Dad. "Periwinkles. Or just 'winkles.' You and Jools can be the mermaids."

"What will you and Mom be?" asked Alix.

"We'll be the mermaid parents," said Dad. "I will be King Neptune."

Alix smiled, then remembered she was feeling sad, and unsmiled.

"You know what else Mrs. Kerr told me?" said Dad.

"What?" asked Alix.

"The icing was also missing from the top of their cinnamon bread," said Dad. "I think that bakery gave you both defective goods. The breakfast cake was tasty, though, even without the icing."

"We ate the icing," said Alix.

"What!" said her dad. "No way!"

"We didn't mean to," said Alix. "We kept snitching little pieces. It was so good. We didn't mean to eat it all."

"Huh," said her dad. "Well, I'll be."

Then he said, "You know what? I think you and Nessa might be secret sisters."

"What do you mean?" asked Alix.

"Secret sisters of the sugary sea," said Dad.

Alix smiled. She couldn't help it.

"It's a little cramped in here," said Dad. "Plus, your shoes make it kind of smelly. What do you say we have some lunch and then go look for periwinkles?"

"Okay," said Alix.

"You might have to help me stand up, though," said her dad. "I don't think I can get unfolded by myself."

"Okay," said Alix. She crawled over him, then took his hand in both of hers and tugged until he could stand up.

"Thanks," he said. "I thought I might be stuck in there forever."

"I thought that, too," said Alix.

It's a little scary to think about at first, but the entire ocean goes up and down. And it's strange to find out that it goes up and down because the sun and the moon are pulling on it, with gravity. But once you realize that it only goes up and down a little bit, and it happens basically the same way every time, over and over again, you get used to the idea and it's completely normal. It's called "tides."

The tides rise and fall a couple of times every day, and there are charts that tell exactly what minute the tide will be highest or lowest. In between, it rises or falls a little, all the time. Like breathing. Very slow breathing.

When the tide is highest, there is not much beach, and when the tide is lowest, there is a lot of beach. There are creatures and plants that live on the part of the shore that is sometimes completely underwater and sometimes out in the open air.

Periwinkles do that. They're about the size of an acorn, rounded and spiraly. The Treffreys stood in the pools and puddles left behind by the tide, picking up the pretty periwinkles and dropping them in their buckets. There were scads of them.

"It's just like u-pick strawberries," said Jools.

"Only different," said Alix. "You can't just pop these in your mouth."

The beach was a different beach. They'd driven to it in the car through a hillier, emptier part of the island. They parked in a wide space alongside the road on top of one of the hills. Two other cars were already there. The way to know it was the right place was there was an old rusty billboard with a peeling picture of a lobster on it.

Behind the billboard, they found the hidden path that led down the steep, wooded hillside to the hidden beach. The beach curved gently forward on both sides, hugged the whole way around by the steep hills. All you could see was the hills, the beach, and the ocean. No hotels or houses or cars or even any other land. Or people. Except for a handful of people way down at one end, who were also bent over with buckets.

Alix picked up another periwinkle and examined it. The part you ate was inside the shell—she knew that. She turned it over and looked at that part. It glistened. She thought she saw it move a little bit.

"I don't think it's ripe yet," she said.

"It doesn't get ripe," said Dad. "It's not a fruit. Well, I guess it's a *fruits de mer*, as they say in France. 'Fruit of the sea.' It's a sea snail."

Jools stood up and looked at him.

"These are snails?" she said. "We're going to eat snails?"

"What did you think they were?" asked Mom.

"I don't know," said Jools. "Little fish, maybe. I didn't really think about it."

"Fish, snails, what's the difference?" asked Dad.

"I don't know," said Jools. "Snails are . . . creepier. I mean, snails are cool, but I don't want to eat one."

Alix gently emptied her bucket onto the rocks.

"Oops," she said. "I dropped mine."

Jools crouched down and eased her periwinkles into a pool of water.

"Oops!" she said. "Mine spilled, too. Oh, well."

"Hey, wait a minute!" said Dad. "What about our Seafood Dinner?"

"I feel like I'm not going to be that hungry tonight," said Alix.

"Me, neither," said Jools. "I had such a big lunch."

"Maybe we could just eat the part of the dinner that's not seafood," said Alix. "Like the bread and butter."

"And the salad," said Jools.

"And dessert," said Alix.

"Suit yourself," said Dad. "But don't come begging for my periwinkles when you see how good they are."

"Or mine," said Mom. "I'm planning to eat loads of them. And they're going to be swimming in butter."

"They're going to be still swimming?" said Jools.

"It's just an expression," said Mom. "There will be lots of melted butter. And garlic, I think. On pasta. It's going to be so good. My mouth is watering just thinking about it."

Alix and Jools were unconvinced.

Looking over Jools's shoulder, Alix saw that some of the other people had meandered their way. Two grown-ups and a boy. The boy looked familiar. Something about the way he moved. Sort of jumpy.

"Hey, Jools," she said, "isn't that Roby-like-Toby?"

"Who?" said Jools.

"You know," said Alix. "That one kid from the seagulls and the potato chips. One was James and one was Roby-like-Toby."

Jools turned to look.

"Yeah," she said. "I think it is.

"Let's go say hi," said Alix. "Is that okay?" she asked, turning to her mom.

"Sure," said Mom. "Go ahead."

So they trotted over to where the boy who looked like Roby stood with his bucket, looking down at the sand.

"Roby?" said Jools.

He looked up.

"Oh," he said. "Hi!" He smiled. "What are you guys doing here?"

"We were looking for periwinkles," said Alix. "But then we found out that they're snails. Now we don't want to eat them. Are you going to eat them?"

"We're vegetarians," said Roby. "Plus I don't even know what one looks like. Does it look like a regular snail?"

"Sort of," said Jools. "Look." She stooped down and pointed to a rock that had lots of them.

"Look close," she said. "Their shells are swirly, just like regular snails."

Roby knelt down and peered at the periwinkles.

"They are, aren't they," he said. "They're kind of pretty."

"So, if you're not looking for periwinkles," said Alix, "what are you looking for?"

"Sea glass," said Roby. He reached into his bucket and fished out a bean-shaped bit of frosty green glass.

"Is it really glass?" asked Jools.

"Yep," said Roby. "It's glass that gets dropped in the ocean somehow and broken into pieces. Then the water and sand tumble the pieces all around until they're smoothed out and frosty."

"That's so cool," said Jools.

"I know," said Roby. "My mom calls them 'mermaid tears.' She makes jewelry out of them. This is a good beach for it, I guess. But still, you don't find a lot. My mom is really good at it, though."

"Hey!" said Alix. "Is this one?" She plucked a fragment of aqua from the wet sand, rinsed it off in a puddle, and showed it to Roby.

"Yeah, that's a good one!" he said.

"Will your mom mind if I keep this one?" she asked.

"It's not *our* beach," said Roby. "Anyone can find them."

"Can we see the other pieces you found?" asked Jools.

"Sure," said Roby. He tipped his bucket and let the pieces fall into his hand. One of them was still shaped like the top of a bottle.

"This won't make very good jewelry," he said. "But I think it's cool."

"I think it would make a good necklace," said Jools. "You could just put a string or a chain right through the hole."

"Here," he said, handing it to her. "You can have it."

"Really?" said Jools.

"Sure," said Roby.

"I'll help you look for more," said Jools. "For your mom."

"Okay," said Roby.

That was so Jools. She was always doing helpful things for people.

Alix decided she would help find sea glass pieces for Roby's mom, too, after she found a few more for herself. And for her friends. She wanted to find one for Rose, and she wanted to find one for Nessa. And maybe one for her own mom. And Jools.

It wasn't as easy as finding the first piece. Or as finding periwinkles. She moved slowly across the sand, searching.

She had almost forgotten what she was looking for

when a glimmer of white caught her eye. She reached down to pick it up and saw, right next to it, a small brown nub. It could have been a pebble, but when she pushed the sand away from around it, she saw that it was an inch-long curvy frosty fragment. The white one was also good. It was flat and had a narrow, elegant shape. Two at once!

She slipped them into the pocket of her shorts and kept looking. She needed one more. Or maybe a few more, so that she could keep some on her dresser at home for decoration and for a souvenir.

And then a green one! Tiny but sweet. It was such a pretty color.

That was it, for a while. It was funny how you could really, really want something that an hour ago you had never heard of. Alix glanced back over her shoulder at Jools and Roby. They weren't even trying. They were just sitting on the sand, talking and laughing. She, Alix, was probably already the champion, out of the three of them.

She kept looking. As if to encourage her, the sand offered up two more bits right away—a light green and a deep blue. She found something that was not glass, but maybe had been part of a dish or a teacup. There was a blue-and-white pattern on one side. And she found what might be a coin. She studied it. It was hard to tell if it was a pirate treasure–type coin, or just a beat-up penny with a weird hole in it.

She decided to show it to her dad, who knew about stuff like that. She saw that both of her parents were now over with Roby's mom and dad, jabbering away. Roby and Jools were running around in a giant circle playing some kind of keep-away game.

Everyone was having a great old time while Alix sifted the sand for bits of trash. But she didn't mind. She liked her bits of trash. And she liked searching for them. Oh, look—another white one. And look—here was a green.

Eventually, she wandered back across the beach. She slipped herself under her mom's arm and wrapped her own arms around her mom's middle. Mom squeezed her, and gave her a pat, talking all the while.

Alix let the grown-ups' talking drift away over her head, like music that plays in a restaurant, in the background.

She let her eyes drift around, too. Jools and Roby were crouched down by the water's edge, inspecting something that Jools held in her cupped hands.

The tide was coming in. A large boulder Alix had walked around earlier now had water up to one side of it.

Her parents' buckets were full to the brim with periwinkles and seawater.

She was just being quiet, noticing things, when she noticed Roby's mom's necklace. Or at least one of her necklaces. She was wearing three or four of them. This one was two pieces of sea glass, one white and one green, with a piece of silver wire wrapped around them, like a cage. A narrow velvet ribbon went through a loop in the silver wire, and around her neck. The ribbon was light green, too.

It looked like something Alix could do.

Jools was in charge of the salad. She had to wash everything off and make it the right size.

Alix's job was to make the garlic bread. She had to spread butter on the bread, sprinkle garlic salt on it, then wrap it up in aluminum foil and put it in the oven. She knew how. She had done it before.

Their parents were busy prying boiled periwinkles out of their shells with toothpicks. This was taking longer than they expected. They hadn't even gotten to the part where they put them on the pasta. But they were laughing and having fun.

Yuck, thought Alix about the periwinkles. She wiped off the counter where she had put together the garlic bread. She folded the plastic bag the bread had come in, and picked up the twist tie. And looked at it. A tiny smidgen of silver was visible at the end of it.

She tried peeling away the paper part of the twist tie to get to the silvery wire. Most of the paper came off, but there was still a plasticky sheath around the wire.

Super-carefully, she set it on the cutting board Jools had been using, and scraped away at it with the paring knife. It worked! Silver wire!

She reached into her pocket and pulled out a piece of the sea glass. She wrapped the silvery wire around it. It just barely went around twice. She was going to need more twist ties.

She found a couple of wrinkled ones in the drawer where the matches and the scissors were, but she needed more. She looked around the small kitchen. Her eyes fell on the trash can. Which had a trash-can liner. Trash-can liners had twist ties sometimes.

Under the sink, she found the box of trash-can liners. Bingo! A whole sheet of twist ties. Good long ones.

"What are you doing in there, Alix?" said her mom.

"Nothing," said Alix. "Just . . . just nothing."

"What kind of nothing?" said her mom.

The oven timer pinged.

"Garlic bread's ready!" said Alix. She slipped the twist ties and the wire-wrapped sea glass into her pocket and wiped the paper shreds from the counter.

She and Jools had garlic bread, salad, and plain pasta with butter and cheese, while Mom and Dad continued to coax periwinkles from shells. They were making progress. The heap of empty shells was growing.

Alix carried the dishes back into the kitchen and stealthily started to de-paper another twist tie. She had to be careful not to cut it in half while she was scraping the paper away. Also not to cut her finger in half.

"What on earth . . . ," said her mother.

Alix hadn't heard her coming.

"Just messing around," said Alix.

"Can I ask why?" asked her mom.

Alix took the piece of sea glass she had wrapped in the silvery wire out of her pocket and set it on the counter. She put the twist ties on the counter, too.

"I want to make necklaces for people," she said. "Like Roby's mom does."

Her mom picked up the wrapped sea glass and admired it.

“This wire is from a twist tie?” she asked.

Alix nodded.

“You are really something else,” said Mom. “What are you going to use for the necklace part, the part that goes around your neck?”

“I don’t know yet,” said Alix. “I was thinking of asking Mrs. Kerr if she had some ribbon, like for wrapping presents.”

“That’s a good idea,” said her mom. “Tell you what, though. I think these twist ties would come in handy for tying up garbage bags. What do you say we go to a hardware store, or a craft store, and get a little spool of wire? And maybe some ribbon?”

This sounded like fun.

“It was going to be a surprise,” said Alix. “I was going to make one for you and Jools and Rose and Nessa.”

“It was a surprise,” said Mom. “I am completely surprised. And it will still be a surprise for everyone else. I won’t tell anyone.”

"Okay," said Alix. On tiptoe, she looked over the half wall between the kitchen and the living room. Jools came into the living room from their bedroom. She had changed into her nightgown. She couldn't have heard anything. Dad was still prying periwinkles from their shells. He wasn't paying attention.

"Okay," said Alix, again. She swept the treasures back into her hand and dropped them into her pocket. Except for the coin, which she had forgotten about.

"Do you think this is old?" she asked her mom.

Her mom examined it.

"I think it's a subway token," she said. "So it's a little bit old but not ancient."

She handed it back to Alix.

Alix said, "Hmm." Then she said, "So, it's probably not real gold, either."

"No," said Mom. "It's not gold. But it's pretty cool to think about how it found its way from someone else's pocket into the ocean and then all the way to you and your pocket."

"I wonder who it was," said Alix. "I hope it was someone good."

"What do you mean, 'good'?" asked Mom.

"Someone interesting," said Alix.

"Everyone is interesting," said Mom.

"Someone really interesting, though," said Alix. "Someone who was going on a big journey, or someone who was trying to make their dreams come true. Or someone who was escaping from something."

"That's exactly who it was," said Mom. "One of those people."

"How do you know?" asked Alix.

"I just do," said Mom.

"I hope this wasn't the only subway token they had," said Alix. "I hope that it didn't ruin their life when they lost it."

"Maybe it saved their life," said Mom. "Maybe it was really lucky they didn't get on the subway that day."

"Wow," said Alix. "I didn't even think of that."

That was a lot of mysteries for one little subway token. It was almost the best kind of treasure.

chapter 6

PINEYWILD

One morning, the Treffreys borrowed the bikes Mrs. Kerr kept behind the house and rode them to a place called PineyWild. They found out about it from the basket of brochures on the surfboard coffee table.

There were brochures for all kinds of things: whale-watching boats and amusement parks and kayaking. And even for parasailing, which was like waterskiing, only up in the air with a parachutey-type thing helping you stay up there. These were all pretty pricey, though. PineyWild was free. And it wasn't that far away, so they hopped on the bikes and headed out.

PineyWild was a wildlife refuge, which sounded exciting. Maybe even dangerous. As Alix pedaled along, she felt a shiver of anticipation.

"What kind of wildlife do you think they have there?" she asked.

"I imagine we'll see quite a few birds," said Mom.

"I'm hoping to see some dragonflies," said Dad.

"Birds," said Jools. "And bugs. No wonder it's free."

Mom laughed.

"I think it will be fun," she said. "Anyhow, it will be interesting."

"Interesting to us, or just interesting to you guys?" asked Jools.

"It'll be great," said Dad. "You'll see."

Alix rode over a bump and looked down to see a flattened-out rabbit whiz by underneath. She let out a yelp that was quickly echoed by Jools as she rode over the dead rabbit, too.

"I guess that one didn't quite make it to the refuge," said Dad, over his shoulder.

"Cal," said Mom, from behind.

"What?" said Dad.

The ride was easy. There were no big hills. Shadows crisped and faded as the sun went in and out of clouds.

The Treffreys pedaled across a bridge over a creek where people were fishing. Farther up the creek, they could see bright spots of color that were kayaks and the T-shirts of whoever was paddling them.

After that, there were fewer houses and more fields, with tangly copses of trees and shrubs. They passed one house, close to the road, with a large gray bird standing on the peak of the roof. It stood on tall, spindly legs with knobby knees, its neck curved into an S.

"What kind of bird is that?" asked Alix. It took off, and she braced herself, half expecting it to dive-bomb them. But it didn't. It flew away.

"It's a heron," said Mom. "A great blue heron. Did you see the pond in the yard? It probably had fish in it. Or frogs."

"I guess some birds are interesting," said Jools. "Kind of."

Before long they coasted into a gravel parking lot. A few cars were there, and some bikes. A large map showed the three main parts of PineyWild.

The closest part had once been a cranberry bog. The middle part, which was the biggest, had once been a golf course. The farthest-away part had once, a hundred years or so ago, been a village.

All the sections of PineyWild had once been one thing, but were going to be something else. Except for the former cranberry bog. That was going to be a cranberry bog again. Maybe. The map said *Proposed Cranberry Bog Restoration*.

The old golf course was a Habitat Restoration Project. Volunteers were yanking out all the plants that had come from somewhere else and planting the kind that had been there in the first place. Then they would let it go kind of wild. This was so the animals, birds, insects, and fish would have the food they needed, plus plenty of nonpoisonous thickets and tangles and trees for nesting and hidey-holes.

"Because," said Mom, "imagine trying to find something to eat or a place to hide on a golf course. Maybe if you were a worm, it would be okay. Or an ant. Or a person, who could go into the clubhouse and order up a sandwich."

The former village would have some gardens and a nature center. It already had a few buildings.

The map was drawn so that the parts of PineyWild that were all finished were solid lines. The parts that weren't finished yet were dotted lines. There were way more dotted lines than solid ones. A lot of PineyWild was still just an idea someone had.

"What a fascinating project," said Dad.

"It's ambitious," said Mom.

"It's mostly imaginary," said Jools.

"Well," said Dad. "It's true that there's a lot of work to do yet. But it's a real place. And there are trails. Let's take a look!"

So they found the opening in the trees where the trail started, and into the wild pines they went.

For a few minutes.

Almost right away, they were out of the woods and into The Once and Future Cranberry Bog. There was an informational sign that said so. While their parents stopped to read it, Alix and Jools went out into the middle of the bog on a boardwalk. The bog looked like a great big old field, except that here and there, glimmers of water could be seen. Including right underneath them, right now.

"How deep do you think it is?" asked Alix.

"I don't think it's that deep," said Jools. "There's grass growing out of it. And flowers. Plus, they built this boardwalk."

"That's true," said Alix. She knelt down to take a closer look.

"Hey, Jools," she said, "do you think these are cranberries?"

"Where?" said Jools. She knelt down, too.

"There," said Alix. She pointed. "They're green, but they could be baby cranberries."

"Maybe," said Jools. "Taste one."

"Should I?" asked Alix. She reached for a berry.

"No!" said Jools. "It might be something poisonous."

"One berry won't kill me," said Alix.

"If it's poisonous," said Jools, "one *drop* could kill you."

Alix opened her mouth and moved the berry closer.

"Alix!" said Jools, sharply. Then she said, "Go ahead—I don't care."

Alix dropped the berry into the water.

"I guess I won't," she said.

About three-quarters of the way across the bog, the boardwalk ended, and there were only loose boards lying end to end. The boards sank slightly into the soggy earth as Alix and Jools stepped on them.

"I guess we're on the dotted line now," said Jools, who was in front.

Clouds of tawny butterflies rose from the sparse bushes as they passed.

And then there weren't even boards, just an ordinary dirt trail leading into the trees.

"We must be at the end of the imaginary cranberry bog," said Alix.

"And," said Jools, as she reached down and stood back up, raising a small, cracked, white ball into the air, "maybe we're at the beginning of the imaginary golf course."

The mosquitoes in the leafy shadows were not imaginary. Fortunately, as Alix and Jools stepped back into the sunshine, the mosquitoes seemed to stay behind.

The trail came to a T at a paved path. A YOU ARE HERE map showed that this path went, roughly, in a giant circle. It showed the different things you might see along the way.

Jools and Alix sat down on a bench to wait for their parents, and Jools studied the map. Alix studied a scab on her knee, and a crack in the pavement with grass growing out of it, and the gently rolling landscape in front of them. She saw a velvety-gray, thumb-sized creature scurry out onto the path, pause, then skitter the rest of the way into the tall grasses on the other side.

"Jools," she said, putting her hand on Jools's arm. But by the time Jools said, "What?" there was nothing to see.

"Nothing," said Alix. "A little animal ran across the path. Like a mouse, but not exactly."

"Dang," said Jools. She would have liked to see it. "I wonder why they stopped having the golf course here."

"Maybe not enough people came to it," said Alix.

"Maybe someone built a newer, better one, and everybody goes there now," said Jools. "Like the mall."

"People are so fickle," said Alix. Because this was what Dad said every time people went to a new place instead of an old place. He liked old places.

"Not all of them," said Jools, who actually knew what *fickle* meant. It meant the opposite of *loyal*.

"Some of them are, though," said Alix, just to keep the conversation going.

"Some of them are what?" asked Dad. He and Mom had arrived.

"Some people are fickle," said Alix.

"But not all of them," said Jools.

"Because they're all going to the new golf course," said Alix, "instead of this one."

"Is there a new golf course?" asked Mom.

"We don't know," said Jools. "There might be."

"Or there might not," said Alix.

"It's a mystery," said Mom.

They decided to go left. The paved path was the old golf cart path. They could still see the old sand traps, and little ponds. But the grass was tall, like a meadow, with black-eyed Susans, goldenrod, milk-weed, and other wildflowers that Alix and Jools didn't know the names of. Bushes and small trees sprouted up. Butterflies and little birds fluttered here and there.

By and by, they came upon a long, low building that slanted to a tall peak in the middle. The tall part was all windows, and the whole building looked modern, until you noticed the peeling wood, the broken rain gutters, and the dangling light fixtures. Weeds flourished between the stones and among the overturned chairs on the patio. Pine trees crowded the edges, as if they were thinking about taking over the patio, too.

"This must have been the clubhouse," said Dad.

The building wore a ribbon of faded yellow tape that said DO NOT ENTER, over and over. But it didn't say DO NOT PEEK, so they went up to the windows and looked in.

Sun poured into the big dining room through a sky-light, which turned out to be not a skylight but a place where the roof was missing. A small tree had somehow taken root in the sunny spot and was finding its way up toward the light.

In the shadows, a table draped in a white cloth held stacks of plates, rows of glasses, and a scattering of brown, dried-up leaves. A banner on the wall said CONGRATULATIONS! to someone. Wilted, silvery balloons drooped from ribbons.

Alix pressed her face to the glass, trying to read the name of who was getting congratulated. She noticed a chandelier resting on a tabletop.

"Creepy," said Jools.

"I wonder how long ago this place closed down," said Dad.

Just then, a mother raccoon with her three raccoonlets waddled into the dining room. She dragged a shiny plastic bag to an open spot on the stained carpet.

Expertly, as if she knew exactly how to do it, she nipped at one side of the bag. She ripped the bag open with her nimble fingers, turned the bag just so, and poured out a small hill of pastel-colored mint candies.

Not the kind that are shaped like M&M's, but the chalky little pillows.

The mother and her cubs gathered around the heap of mints. They each selected a mint and began to eat, in tiny bites, like princesses at a tea party.

"At least they'll have fresh breath," said Mom.

The raccoons looked up at the sound of her voice and gazed at the snooping humans. But they didn't stop chewing. Before long, their attention returned to their feast. The Treffreys watched for a few minutes more, then left the abandoned clubhouse and headed back along the path.

By this point, Alix and Jools did not expect a lot from PineyWild. It was just going to be a walk. A boring walk through deserted places.

The good part about that was how, when you were desperate, little things could seem interesting. Like how the heat made a shimmery place in the air. Or how ants were building giant sand hills in the cracks of the pavement.

The raccoons had been the best so far. How they held those mints in their little hands. Their furry faces.

"The baby ones were so cute," said Alix. "I wonder if you can have a raccoon for a pet."

"I think they have rabies sometimes," said Jools.

"Well, you would get shots for it," said Alix, "like a dog or a cat."

"I think they can be mean," said Jools.

"Do you know that, or do you just think that?" said Alix.

"I think it," said Jools. "But I think I heard it somewhere."

"I don't think Trevor would like it anyway," said Alix. "I think he likes being an only pet."

Jools agreed. Alix could tell that Jools didn't really like the idea of a pet raccoon, but she wasn't sure why. Maybe she was afraid of them. Jools was afraid of things sometimes. Even of doing things. Mom called it "being cautious." "There's nothing wrong with that," she said.

Alix was cautious, too, now and then. But she usually went ahead and did the things anyway.

Up ahead, their parents had stopped to read another sign. A couple of other people were reading it, too, and a few more were approaching from the opposite direction. Then they were all talking, and Dad was pointing off to the left. The other people went where he had pointed, while Mom and Dad gestured to Jools and Alix to hurry up.

"What do you think it is?" said Alix, as they trotted along.

"Who knows?" said Jools. "Something that doesn't exist, probably."

"There's a raptor center here," said Dad. "I didn't notice it on the big map. But it's right down this path, and there's a tour that starts in ten minutes."

"A what?" said Jools.

"A raptor center!" said Dad. "Hawks! Owls! Birds of prey!"

"I thought a raptor was a kind of dinosaur," said Alix.

They were all hurrying along now.

"It can be," said Dad. "But in this case, it's hawks and owls and stuff. Wouldn't you like to see a hawk, close up?"

"Um, maybe?" said Jools. It wasn't something she had thought about. At all. Ever.

The path led them to a dirt road through a scruffy woods. Before long, they came to a clearing and a small community of little cabins. When they got close, they could see that many of the cabin walls weren't solid. They were made of a couple of layers of sturdy wire mesh. You could see through them. The people who had already arrived stood peering through the screen into the first cabin.

"Is this it?" asked Alix.

"I think it might be," said Dad.

Alix noticed that aside from a baby sleeping in a front pack and a toddler who had just been unloaded from his dad's backpack, she and Jools were the only two people in the "youth" category. It was all grown-ups. She prepared to shift into things-that-are-mostly-interesting-to-old-people mode. But before she could fully readjust, the toddler dad turned toward the Treffreys with a big smile on his face and motioned to them to come and see.

When they did, they saw a white bird the size of a fire hydrant calmly sitting on a post. It looked right back at them, with round yellow eyes.

"Snowy owl," said the toddler dad.

Without moving its body, the snowy owl spun its head halfway around, then back. A few seconds later, it did the same thing in the other direction.

"It has to do that," said a white-haired woman with binoculars hanging around her neck. "It can't move its eyes, so it has to turn its whole head to see around it."

Alix tried this briefly—looking straight ahead and moving her head around to see. It seemed like a lot of work.

"So, is this like a zoo?" asked Jools. "For birds?"

"Not exactly," said a voice. They all turned to see a slender woman with silvery braids. She wore rubber boots over her jeans and a leather glove that went part-way up her arm.

"Hi," she said. "I'm Sara."

She explained that this was a place where people

took care of sick and injured raptors until they could return to their normal life in the wild. A raptor was a bird of prey, a bird that hunted. It could be small, like a kestrel, or huge, like an eagle.

There were many ways raptors might be injured. They could fly into a power line or be hit by a car. It was hard to be a raptor in a world full of humans, with all their wires and buildings and machines. Sometimes, humans even did stuff to birds on purpose, like knock the babies out of trees so they could try to have them as pets. This wasn't a good idea. Also, it was against the law.

But humans could do good things for birds, too. Like make wildlife refuges. And raptor centers.

If birds were going to be released into the wild again, it wasn't good for them to be around people too much. So the birds Sara was showing them were "educational" birds, birds that wouldn't survive on their own.

For example, the snowy owl had lost some parts of

his wing that could never grow back. He could fly a little bit, but not enough.

Alix was next to the toddler dad, who was holding both of his son's hands. Every twenty seconds or so, the little boy would pick up both feet at the same time and hang from his father's hands, to entertain himself. The dad was doing an excellent job of listening to Sara without letting the kid fall on the ground.

Sara showed them a sweet tiny owl and a hawk. Every bird had its own cabin, which was called a "mew." This might seem lonely, but actually, the raptors liked it that way. They weren't social birds.

There were also bigger cabins, called "flight pens," where birds could practice flying again.

Lulu was a peregrine falcon who had been hit by a truck. She was blind in one eye and deaf in one ear, so hunting for food would be very hard for her. Sara was training Lulu to fly over and perch on her arm that had the long glove on it. Lulu came over because Sara was holding food between her thumb and her other fingers. Lulu sat there calmly, pulling the food out and chomping.

Just then, an older boy, maybe in high school, ran

up and said, "Excuse me, Sara. Sorry to interrupt, but there's a bird coming in."

"When?" asked Sara.

"Right now," said the boy. "Guy found it on the side of the road."

"Oh," said Sara. "Okay. Thanks, Teddy."

"I'll go get everything ready," said Teddy. And he ran off again.

Sara tilted Lulu toward a perch, and Lulu stepped onto it.

"So," said Sara. "A bonus! Now you all get to see what we do when a bird comes in."

As she led them to a small building that was half hidden by flowers and vines, they heard the rumble of an approaching car. A jeep pulled into the clearing. A man jumped out, went around to the passenger side, and started to haul out a large cardboard box. Sara helped him carry the box into the building. Everyone crowded in after them, trying not to get in the way. This was tricky, because there wasn't much space. The adults let Alix and Jools be in front, so they could see. The toddler was on his dad's hip now. The baby was awake, but interested in other things.

Sara lifted a bird carefully from the cardboard box and laid it gently on a blanket, on a table. The bird lay quite still, but quivering, as she sprayed something all over it.

"It looks like Lulu," said Alix, softly.

"That's right," said Sara. "This is a peregrine falcon, just like Lulu."

She wrapped the bird up snugly in the blanket, as if it were a baby, and said to Alix, "Would you like to hold it for a few minutes?"

Alix couldn't believe it. She looked up at her mom and dad.

"Go ahead, honey," said Dad.

Sara told her to sit down on the bench next to the wall, and before she knew it, her arms were filled with bundled-up bird. All she could really see was the bird's face: the sharp hooked beak, the big dark eyes, and the feathers around them. She saw its eyelids. And its eyelashes. The rest of it was covered up by the blanket. But she could feel its fast breathing, its racing heart. She could feel the warm, stunned, trembling weight of it in her lap.

The falcon looked her right in the eye.

Sara was talking to the others, but Alix was paying attention to the bird. She spoke softly to it, and it listened. At least it seemed to.

"You're going to be okay," said Alix. "Everything's going to be okay."

The falcon blinked.

"I know," said Alix. "What's happening now is very weird. It feels kind of weird to me, too. But it's good. Sara's going to help you. She'll help you to fly again. Fly, fly, fly. Fly away home."

She kept saying comforting things while Sara knelt down and worked a plastic tube between the top and bottom of the bird's beak. The tube was connected to a syringe. Sara gently squeezed fluid into the bird.

"Mmm," said Alix to the falcon. "Yum, yum."

Sara smiled.

"Lactated Ringer's solution," she said. "So tasty!"

She lifted the bird from Alix's arms back to the table. She unwrapped it and, with Teddy's help, examined it. The bird let them. As Alix watched, along with the others, she could still feel its weight and its warmth, its heartbeat and breathing, in her arms.

Sara said the bird didn't seem to have any broken bones.

"Maybe it's just stunned," she said. "We'll take it to one of our veterinarians to make sure."

She wrapped the blanket around the falcon again, lifted it carefully into the bottom half of a pet travel crate, and then put the top on.

"And now," she said, "If you'll excuse me, I need to make some phone calls and see who's available to help us out. Feel free to visit all the birds again. Teddy will be out there to try to answer any questions that you have. Thanks so much for visiting us!"

She signaled to Teddy, who went over and held the door open for people to file out.

As Alix passed Sara, she said, "Thank you for letting me hold the falcon."

Sara smiled. "Thank you for holding it," she said. "You did a great job."

"I hope it's okay," said Alix.

"I think it will be," said Sara.

Alix skipped to catch up with Mom, Dad, and Jools, who were already outside. They visited each bird again: the tiny owl; the hawk; Lulu, the peregrine falcon; and the snowy owl, whose name was Alonzo. There was also a turkey vulture, which they hadn't seen before. That one was really strange looking. A little, red, featherless head poked out of its fluffy black neck.

Alix thought it was kind of ugly. But then it turned its wrinkly head and looked at her. The curiosity in its eye made it seem more handsome. It seemed to say, "I am a living creature, not just a weird thing to look at."

She had never looked into the eyes of so many birds before. The falcon had been extra-close-up, plus she had been actually holding it. She didn't even have words to describe what that was like.

Now, holding the gaze of the turkey vulture felt almost normal. Maybe she was becoming a Bird Girl. Then the turkey vulture looked away. So maybe she wasn't.

As they headed back down the dirt road, Jools asked, "So, was it scary, holding the falcon?"

"It was the most amazing feeling ever," said Alix.

"I bet," said Jools. "I bet it was. But a little bit scary."

"A little bit scary," said Alix. "But not too. Do you wish you got to hold it?"

"No," said Jools. "I'm glad it was you."

Alix wondered if she would ever be as mature as Jools. Because she was pretty sure she would always want to be the one who got to hold the falcon.

At the hundred-years-ago village, there was only one small building. What had looked like buildings on the big map were just the stone outlines of buildings that had been there once upon a time. The foundations were all that was left.

But it wasn't creepy like the golf-course clubhouse

with the shriveled balloons and the dead leaves on the white tablecloth. Some of the foundations had grass growing inside, and in others, the PineyWild people were making different kinds of gardens. So far, there was a food garden, a butterfly garden, an herb garden, and a backyard wildlife-refuge garden.

The idea was that you could go home and make these kinds of gardens in your own backyard.

Today, they were working on the butterfly garden. Two people were digging out a hole for a pond, and two others were making a path out of bricks. This would be a garden with a lot of flowers, because that's what butterflies need.

"What do you say, Viv," said Dad. "Shall we go home and turn our yard into a wildlife refuge?"

"We could maybe do a little something," said Mom. "Here and there."

"I think I like the butterfly one," said Jools.

"Maybe we could do some of each," said Alix. "I like the archy thing with the vines growing over it."

"Could we have a pond?" asked Jools.

"With lily pads?" added Alix. "And a bridge over it?"

"How about a birdbath?" said Mom. "With flowers around it?"

"How about a cranberry bog?" said Dad. "It would be the only one in Shembleton, I bet."

"That's not even one of the ones they're saying to do," said Jools. She didn't want a cranberry bog in the backyard. "A pond is kind of in between a bog and a birdbath."

"Then maybe we would have a heron on our roof," said Alix. "Watching our pond."

"I don't think every pond has a heron," said Jools. She didn't know why she all-of-a-sudden wanted a pond in the backyard. She just did. And she felt that the story of her life was wanting a pond and getting a birdbath. Or a bog.

Though maybe it wasn't the story of her life. Maybe she was just hungry.

Outside the small building, which was bathrooms,

there was a vending machine. All it had was healthy snacks, but they got some to tide them over until they found some real food.

Seeds and nuts when you wanted real food.

A birdbath instead of a pond.

Same thing.

As they continued down the trail, Jools started a list of all the things she felt crabby about. She included recent complaints and long-ago grievances and annoying things that might happen in the future.

Recent: breakfast cake with all of the icing pulled off. By Alix.

Long ago: how when Alix got glasses, she insisted on getting the exact same kind as Jools.

Future: Alix was sure to do something annoying. Who could predict what it would be?

Across the field, through a gap in the trees, she glimpsed the peaked roof of the falling-apart clubhouse. So they must be getting close to the parking lot where their bikes were.

Good, she thought. *Good riddance.* She was glad they were almost done with PineyWild. PineyWild was dumb. She wanted a pond. And she wanted to hold the falcon.

Or at least, she wished she wanted to hold the falcon. She wanted to be the one who did a brave thing. An adventure-y thing. The feeling kept growing in her, all the way back to the parking lot. So that when they finally got there, and Dad said, "Who wants to ride all the way to the lighthouse?" it was Jools who said, "I do!"

She didn't expect both Mom and Alix to say that they were tired, and they just wanted to go back to Mrs. Kerr's. When they did, she almost said, "Me, too." But her small candle of boldness stayed lit.

She said, "See you later, then." And climbed onto her bike. And rode off. Just like that.

Mom and Alix weren't really too tired. They had a secret mission. Once Jools and Dad rode off, Mom pulled out her phone and asked it to lead them to the craft store.

It turned out that the craft store was in the same bunch of shops as the bakery. It was right across the street.

The inside of the craft store was a cluttery jumble. Alix and Mom made their way through bins of fat yarn, tubs of artificial flowers, and shelves of wooden objects waiting to be painted. They stopped to look at tiny people and cows and furniture and trees that were for model-train scenery. There were trees for every season: the autumn trees were sponges, painted orange and yellow; the winter ones were twigs, frosted with white glitter. There were ponds, made of something that looked like water, but it was hard.

"Look," said Alix, "a pond for Jools!"

"Oh, look at that," said Mom. She touched the hard part with her fingertip and looked into its depths. "Why are we here again? I've completely forgotten."

"Wire and ribbon," said Alix. "For my necklaces."

"Oh," said Mom. "Right. Let's see."

They wandered through picture frames, colored paper, and beads before, by pure luck, Alix spotted a spool of perfect silvery wire.

Ribbon was nearby. There were so many kinds:

velvet and satin, narrow and wide, all colors, stripes, polka dots, and plaid. Alix chose a narrow velvety one, the same light green as one of the pieces of sea glass. It was the just like the ribbon in Roby's mom's necklace. She could hardly believe she got to use it, too. It was so elegant.

They figured out how much they would need for each necklace and how many necklaces there would be.

"Is it too expensive?" Alix asked.

"It's a little pricey," said Mom. "But how about if this is your souvenir?"

"Okay," said Alix.

They paid for the ribbon and wire, then went across the street and got little pastries with ham and cheese in them from the bakery. They ate them at one of the tables with flowers, under the striped awning. Even so, they got back to 4242 Oceanview before Dad and Jools.

"I think they'll be awhile," said Mom. "They were going in the other direction."

So they took out the wire and ribbon and set to

work. Once they figured out how to wrap the wire around the sea glass and make a loop for the ribbon to slip through, Alix made all of them by herself. The very tiny green piece of sea glass was too tiny. She couldn't wrap the wire tight enough to keep it from falling out. She decided to keep it for herself for good luck. She would keep it in her special box on her dresser at home.

She laid the necklaces out in a row on the red table and called to her mom to come and see.

There were seven of them.

"You, Jools, Rose, Nessa, and me," she said. "That leaves two."

"How about Dad?" said Mom.

"He doesn't wear necklaces," said Alix.

"True," said Mom. "Hey, how about Mrs. Kerr?"

"Okay," said Alix. "That's a really good idea."

That left one. Alix looked around the room. The

PineyWild brochure was still opened up on the coffee table, and she remembered how it had seemed boring at first. And then they saw the raccoons having their mint party. And then she got to hold the falcon.

"Mom," she said. "I want to give one to Sara. The bird lady."

"Oh!" said Mom. "That's a really good idea, too."

"Can we go there again, so I can give it to her? Before we go home?"

"Sure," said Mom. "We can do that. It's only ten minutes away in the car."

Alix thought about how raptors, which she had thought were dinosaurs, were also birds. And how the horseshoe crabs, which she had never even heard of, had been in the ocean since before dinosaurs. Periwinkles, which she had also never heard of, were sea snails. Animals needed hidey-holes and certain kinds of food, and you could tell how high the water rose at high tide by how flat or fluffy the sand was.

It was all so nature-y.

"You and Dad are always trying to teach us things," she said.

"We hardly have to," said Mom. "You keep learning them all by yourselves."

Jools loved her necklace. Alix let her pick which one she wanted. She picked the aqua one. She put it on right away.

"Was the lighthouse fun?" asked Alix.

"It was pretty good," said Jools. "We climbed all the way to the top and looked out. I didn't really like going up. There were one hundred and eighty-two steps, and they went around and around, and they kept getting narrower. They got really narrow. They were metal, with holes that you could see through, and if you leaned over, you could see all the way to the bottom. It made me nervous. But I thought about you, and I kept going."

"You thought about me?" said Alix.

"I thought about how you would go all the way, right to the top, if you were there," said Jools. "I wanted to be someone who would go all the way to the top, too. So I did. And once we got up there, it was cool to look around."

"You wanted to be like me?" said Alix. This was such a new idea.

Jools just nodded.

"The best part," she said, "was that there was a museum in the house that went with the lighthouse, where the lighthouse keeper and his family lived. That was a long time ago, because it's all automatic now. But all the furniture is there from the last lighthouse keeper. So I looked in the rooms, while Dad looked at a bunch of exhibits about how the lighthouse worked.

"One of the rooms was a kid's room. There was a quilt on the bed, and there were books on the shelves. There were even clothes hanging in the closet. I don't know if they were the real girl's clothes or not.

"There was a picture of her on the wall, holding a

cat. She looked like she was my age. Maybe a little older than me. Her name was Carol, like a Christmas carol.

"We weren't supposed to touch anything, but no one else was in there. So I sat on the bed and looked out the window and pretended it was my room. It was a little room. I could reach the bookshelf from the bed. I saw that she had *The Magic Friend*, that book about the boy who accidentally gets on a spaceship going to another galaxy and doesn't see anyone for hundreds of years, and I pulled it out. Her name was on the inside. And a piece of paper, like a bookmark, fell in my lap.

"There was writing on it. It said, 'Who will be my magic friend?' It made me think how living there might be kind of lonely. Not as lonely as a spaceship, but maybe there weren't any other kids around. There was a desk, with some pencils in a can, so I took one and wrote, 'I will.' I put the paper back in the book, and I put the book back on the shelf."

"Do you think she'll know?" asked Alix.

"I don't know," said Jools. "I just liked doing it."

"I think she'll know," said Alix.

"She's probably really old now," said Jools. "Or even dead."

"I still think she'll know," said Alix.

"Maybe," said Jools. "I just liked doing it."

chapter 7

THE LAST DAY

When Alix woke up, she looked over at Jools, who she wanted to be like, but who had also wanted to be like her. At least, for a few seconds.

Jools was still asleep, so Alix peeled out of bed and tiptoed to the kitchen end of the big room. She could hear her parents talking out on the screened porch, so she made herself a bowl of cereal and went out there, too. They were drinking coffee. As usual.

"I can't believe it's our last day," said Mom.

"Then it's back to the old grind," said Dad. "I

don't mind the old grind, though. I like it. But this has been pretty great."

"Today is a Nessa day," said Alix.

"She's already here," said Mom. "I'm surprised you didn't hear her."

Alix was surprised, too. She must have been zonked.

"Listen," said Mom. "Let's go give your necklace to Sara right away, so we can come back and have a good long beach day."

"Okay," said Alix. "But what if she's not there yet?"

"Then we'll leave it with a note," said Mom.

"Okay," said Alix. Though she hoped Sara would be there.

"I wonder how the falcon is," she said.

"Maybe we'll find out," said Mom.

Alix finished her cereal and carried the bowl to the sink.

Back in the bedroom, Jools slept on. Alix changed into her shorts and brushed her teeth. She picked out a necklace, put it in her pocket, and went back out to the porch.

"Ready," she said.

Mom was comparing the map on her phone to the PineyWild brochure, finding the road that went right to the raptor place so they didn't have to walk through the cranberry bog and the golf course.

"Okay," she said. "I think I've got it. Let's go!"

When they arrived at the raptor center, Sara was putting food in Alonzo's cabin. His mew.

"Hey!" she said. "You're back! You're not going to believe this, but I was just thinking about you. It's amazing that you're here right now."

"Really?" said Mom. "Why?"

"Well," said Sara, "remember the peregrine falcon who came in while you were here? The one you held?"

She said this to Alix.

"Yes," said Alix. How could she forget?

"It turned out that he wasn't badly hurt," said Sara. "Just stunned. A minor head injury. He probably had a massive headache, but he just needed a safe place to rest for a day. I'm about to release him. Would you like to do it?"

"Um," said Alix. "Okay, I guess. But I don't know how."

"Of course you don't," said Sara. "I'll show you. It's pretty awesome."

"Okay," said Alix.

"And it would be really great," said Sara to Mom, "if you could take pictures."

"Absolutely!" said Mom.

Alix and Mom followed Sara to the building where Alix had held the falcon. Sara found a camera for Mom and a pair of handling gloves, just like her own, for Alix. The gloves felt big on Alix's hands and went not quite up to her elbows.

Sara led them out through a back door to another mew. They hadn't seen this one yesterday. Just beyond the mew was a small meadow, encircled by trees. Inside the mew was the falcon, sitting on a low branch. He looked different today. He looked alert.

"This is one of our guest mews," said Sarah. "We don't usually name birds unless they're going to stay here. But I've been calling this guy Henry. I don't know why. He just seemed like a Henry."

Henry watched Sara as she entered the enclosure. She wasn't looking back at him; at least she didn't seem to be. She didn't even seem to notice him. Her body was sideways to him, and she seemed to be examining something on one of her gloves.

The bird glanced away, and in that instant Sara grabbed both of his legs and tucked him into her arms, as if she did it every day. Because probably, she did.

"Can you open the door for me?" she asked.

Mom opened it and Sara stepped out with Henry.

"We'll just go out to the middle of the meadow," she said.

It wasn't far, not at all, but Alix had time to get nervous. She looked over at Henry, whom Sara held close in front of her, by his legs, facing forward. Sara made it look easy, but the falcon was large. And wild. He wasn't frightened and wrapped up anymore, and his beak was sharp and pointy. He was looking around, seeing what was what. He looked right at Alix. She did not feel like the Bird Girl.

"Hi," she said. "Remember me? I'm your friend."

"Don't worry," said Sara. "I'll be helping you."

Alix looked at her mom, who smiled, but Alix wondered if she was a little nervous, too.

In the middle of the meadow, they stopped. Sara stood beside Alix and somehow transferred Henry from her own gloved hands to Alix's. It was the strangest feeling: the weight of the bird, his closeness between her arms in front of her, his legs in her hands. There was a different kind of aliveness in him today. Today's kind of aliveness wanted to escape and be free. Alix wasn't sure she could hold on to him for very long.

"Perfect," said Sara. "Now, I'm going to say, 'three, two, one, release!' And when I say, 'release!' you just lift both arms up in front of you, like this, and let go. Don't worry. Henry will know exactly what to do. Are you ready?"

Alix didn't feel ready, not at all, but she nodded.

"Are you ready?" Sara asked Mom, who also nodded. She held up the camera, her finger poised.

"Okay," said Sara. "Here we go: three, two, one, release!"

Alix raised her arms. She let go with her hands. The weight of the falcon lifted. The falcon realized he was free and raised his magnificent wings. He flapped them and started to rise. He dipped a little, then lifted higher. Mom was still taking pictures.

"Good-bye, Henry," said Alix. "Have a happy life!"

"Is that the most beautiful thing you've ever seen, or what?" said Sara.

They watched the falcon soar over the tops of the trees. They could see him flying back and forth, and then he disappeared. He was gone. They watched the empty sky for a minute.

It had happened so fast.

"I want to do it again," said Alix. "Now that I know how."

Sara laughed.

"Well, we don't have anyone else to release right now," she said, "but maybe someday you'll be able to."

They turned to walk back. And then Alix remembered why they had come in the first place. She had almost forgotten.

"I brought something for you," she said. She reached into her pocket and pulled out the sea-glass necklace.

"I made it," she said. "I found the sea glass at the beach."

"Oh, my!" said Sara. She took the necklace and looked closely at it.

"I love it!" she said. "Thank you so much." She put it on, then asked, "Is that why you came here today?"

"Yes," said Alix. "I wanted to thank you for letting me hold the falcon. Henry. I never did it before."

Sara laughed.

"Not too many people have," she said. "But it's pretty special, right?"

Alix nodded.

"I was a little bit scared," she said. "And I was a little bit scared, letting him go."

"But you did it," said Sara. "I knew you could, because I watched you hold him yesterday. I could tell you would rise to the occasion."

"She's a riser-to-the-occasion, this one," said Mom. "That's for sure."

Jools, meanwhile, woke up. She pulled her knees up to her chest and wondered why her legs felt sore. Then she remembered: all that walking, plus the long bike ride, and then the stairs at the lighthouse.

She thought about Carol, the lighthouse girl, and her cat. She wondered how many times Carol climbed the one hundred and eighty-two steps to the top. She wondered if the cat ever did. She imagined Carol opening her book, taking out the bookmark, and finding the message from her, Jools, Girl from the Future. It was like one of the stories she might read. Or maybe, she thought, a story she might write. She found her sketchpad and her pencils, then she crawled back into bed and began.

When Alix told Jools about releasing the falcon, Jools was still writing. She looked up and listened, then said, "That's kind of amazing!" And she meant it.

"Do you wish it was you?" asked Alix.

"Maybe a little," she said. "But I'm glad it was you."

"How do you be so mature?" asked Alix.

Jools shrugged.

"I just like different stuff than you," she said. "Go away so I can finish my story."

So Alix did. But she still wanted to talk about Henry the falcon. She ran upstairs to tell Mrs. Kerr and Nessa. And to give them their necklaces.

She knocked on the door frame and squinted in through the screen. Something smelled good.

"Come right in," said Mrs. Kerr.

Nessa was having lunch. She had a plate of little, crispy, golden fried things, maybe mushrooms, and she was dipping them in ketchup.

"I love fried things dipped in ketchup," said Alix.

"I could eat cardboard if it was fried and dipped in ketchup."

"Then you shall have some," said Mrs. Kerr. "Have a seat."

Several crispy, golden fried things rested on paper towels on the counter. Mrs. Kerr put them on a pretty blue plate and set it in front of Alix.

"I don't want to eat all of yours," said Alix.

"No worries," said Mrs. Kerr. "I've already had mine."

"And I'm on seconds," said Nessa.

Alix squeezed a puddle of ketchup onto her plate. She dipped a fried thing into it and popped it into her mouth. Mmm. A perfect, warm, savory-salty, chewy-crispy combo. And tasty.

"Iced tea?" asked Mrs. Kerr.

Alix nodded. She chewed and swallowed and said, "Yes, please."

Mrs. Kerr brought her a glass of tea, then sat down with them.

"So, what have you been up to?" asked Mrs. Kerr.

Alix told them all about Henry. And she gave them the necklaces.

"This is so cool!" said Nessa.

"How lovely," said Mrs. Kerr. "Thank you so much!"

"I think this is my new favorite food," said Alix. "What is it called?"

"Winkles," said Mrs. Kerr. "Periwinkles. Didn't you have some the other day?"

Alix stopped chewing.

"I'm eating periwinkles?" she said.

"Of course," said Mrs. Kerr.

I have a snail in my mouth, thought Alix. And a bunch more snails are in my stomach.

"I want to hear more about the falcon," said Mrs. Kerr. "Was he content to let you hold him?"

Alix swallowed, so she could speak. Then, without thinking, she popped another periwinkle into her mouth. It was still delicious. Mostly breading and ketchup. But also a little ocean-y.

That afternoon, while Jools was burying Alix and Nessa in the sand so that only their heads stuck out, James and Roby showed up. James wanted to be buried so that only his head stuck out, too. It would look like they were standing up, which would have been a really deep hole to dig, but they were sitting down, all scrunched up, so it wasn't that deep or big.

Or it would look like just heads, without bodies, sitting on the beach like bowling balls.

Jools and Roby packed the sand down firmly around the heads.

Then they looked at each other, smiled, and ran off, laughing.

"Hey!" yelled the three heads.

But Jools and Roby kept running. A little ways up the beach, they sat down. Alix was glad that Jools

had a friend who hadn't been dead for fifty years, but she didn't want to be stuck in the sand forever.

"Jeez," said James. "I thought Roby was my friend."

Alix looked behind her.

"What if we're still here when the tide comes in?" she said.

"Holy crap!" said James. "We could die!"

"Just wiggle your shoulders," said Nessa. She was already wiggling hers. Alix and James started wiggling theirs, too.

"And then rock back and forth," said Nessa, and they all did. It took some work, but they worked themselves free.

"What can we do back to them?" said Alix.

The big hole they had been sitting in was still there.

James thought they should cover it with a towel and get Jools and Roby to run over it and fall in.

"They aren't going to run onto a towel," said Alix. "They'd go around it. But what if we dig the hole under where their towels are now, and then when they go to sit down, they fall in?"

"You guys," said Nessa. "This is dumb. Let's just do something else."

Alix and James didn't think it was that dumb, but before they could get any further with their plans, a blaring electronic voice interrupted them. It was a guy lifeguard, talking through a megaphone. He was telling everyone to get out of the water. Then he and the other lifeguard, who was a girl, were pushing the big rowboat into the waves. They jumped in and started rowing away from the shore. Everyone stopped in their tracks to watch them go.

They rowed up and over the waves, out and away over the swells.

"What are they doing?" asked James. "Where are they going?"

"They must be rescuing someone," said Nessa.

"Is someone drowning?" asked Alix.

"Sometimes people just go out too far," said Nessa. "And then they need help to get back."

"What's going on?" asked Jools.

Alix turned, and saw that Jools and Roby were back. She made a face.

"Sorry," said Jools.

"Not sorry," said Roby, grinning.

"It's not funny," said James. "Someone could be drowning out there."

"We don't really know," said Nessa. "But it looks like they're coming back already."

The water's edge was lined with people. As the boat

bobbed closer, they could see that a third person was in there, wrapped in a blanket. The person was sitting up. She was a girl. A teenager.

The lifeguards jumped out, and pushed and tugged their boat back up onto the sand. They looked so strong. Strong, but also gentle. They helped the girl climb out. They walked with their arms around her to a mother and father who came forward, their arms outstretched.

"Nothing to see here, folks," said the girl lifeguard. "Everyone's fine."

Alix caught a glimpse of the rescued girl as she moved from the lifeguards' arms to her parents' embrace. Her hair was wet, of course. Her head was down, and she held her hand in front of her face, like she didn't want to look at anyone, or anyone to look at her. Alix could only really see her wrist, which had about a dozen bracelets on it, friendship bracelets and other kinds.

The lifeguards talked to her and her parents for a few minutes, and then the parents led her away, up among the umbrellas.

"I bet she was so scared," said Roby. "I would have been. I don't even like being at the deep end of the pool."

"Do you know how to swim?" asked Jools.

"Yeah, sort of," he said. "But I'm not very good at it."

"Let's play Frisbee," said James. "I'll go get mine."

He was off like a shot and back before they could blink.

That was how he played Frisbee, too. Fast. Kind of hyper. He was a wild flinger. It took a lot of running, jumping, and reaching to catch James's tosses. Sometimes you just couldn't do it. When he flung one up into where all the people were, Alix trudged up after it. She hoped it hadn't hit anybody. She was relieved to see that it had landed on an open patch of sand. But it was awfully close to a girl in a beach chair, with a big towel wrapped around her like a long skirt.

"Sorry," said Alix, as she picked up the Frisbee.

"It's okay," said thc girl. She lifted her hand in an "it's okay" gesture, and it had about a dozen bracelets on it: friendship bracelets and other kinds.

She was the rescued girl. She was drinking a can of pop.

"Hey," said Alix. "Are you okay?"

"I'm fine," said the girl. But she didn't seem that fine.

Alix knelt down on the sand.

"Was it scary?" she asked.

"It was," said the girl. "I was pretty freaked out. But I'm fine now. I just feel really stupid."

"Why do you feel stupid?" asked Alix.

"I don't know," said the girl. "I shouldn't have gone out so far by myself. All of a sudden, I couldn't touch the bottom anymore. And then I panicked."

"Everyone makes mistakes," said Alix.

"True," said the girl. "But everyone doesn't need to be rescued by lifeguards."

"A lot of people must," said Alix. "Or they wouldn't be there."

"True," said the girl, again.

"Do you want to know the really stupid thing that I did?" asked Alix.

"Sure," said the girl. "What did you do?"

So Alix told her about how she ate all the icing and nuts from the top of the breakfast cake, walking home from the bakery.

The girl laughed.

"That's really funny," she said.

Alix laughed, too. It hadn't seemed funny to her before, but now it did.

"I guess it is, kind of," she said. Then she said, "Well, I better go play Frisbee. I'm glad you didn't drown."

"You and me both," said the girl. "Thanks for the laugh."

"Bye," said Alix.

"Bye," said the girl. She was smiling.

So was Alix.

On her way back to her friends, she trotted past her parents' blanket. Mom was stretched out on her stomach, her ankles crossed. Dad sat in his beach chair beside her, his hand resting gently on her back. He smiled at Alix as she ran by. She smiled back. Everyone was happy. The sun was shining. The afternoon went on and on until it stopped, but it never stopped being perfect.

The evening was going to be fun, too. Mom and Dad were going out. Mrs. Kerr and Nessa were coming downstairs. They were ordering pizza. Alix and Jools studied the take-out menu, even though they would probably just get the plain kind.

Mom showered and did her hair and put on makeup. Alix and Jools couldn't believe how beautiful she looked, even in her bathrobe.

"Wow, Mom!" said Jools.

"Wait till you see my new dress," said Mom. She went into the bedroom and came out a few minutes later to inspect herself in the mirror between the two rooms.

"It's really beautiful, Mom," said Alix. And it was: it was crisp and slim, with scallops around the scoopy neck.

Mom smiled, pleased. Until she turned around and

looked back over her shoulder into the mirror. Then she groaned.

"Where's your father?" she said. "I'm going to brain him."

Because when Dad had his hand on her back while she fell asleep in the sun, it left a hand shape in her suntan, right between the straps of her going-out dress.

"No one will even notice it, Mom," said Jools.

"I think it looks cool," said Alix. "I wish we were staying another day, so I could get one, too."

"This is the only dress I brought," said Mom.

"Don't brain Dad, Mom," said Jools.

"What does that even mean?" asked Alix.

"You could wear your windbreaker over it," suggested Jools.

"Wouldn't that look glamorous," said Mom. The way she said it meant that it wouldn't look glamorous. Not at all.

"Why do you have to get dressed up?" asked Alix. "Where are you guys going?"

"To dinner," said Mom. "And then to a casino. It's like board games for grown-ups. And card games."

"That sounds fun," said Jools. "Hey, Alix, we could do that here, too. When Mrs. Kerr and Nessa come down."

"Okay," said Alix. "Do we have to get dressed up?"

"No," said Jools.

"We can wear our necklaces," said Alix.

"Okay," said Jools.

Sometime later, Alix, Jools, and Nessa sat at the kitchen table playing cards, in their nightgowns. And their necklaces. Mrs. Kerr was over in the big comfy chair, watching television. By and by, she came over to the kitchen for a glass of water.

"What are you playing?" she asked.

"Casino," said Jools.

"That's why we're wearing our necklaces," said Alix. "See?"

"Ah, yes," said Mrs. Kerr. "Very fancy. What card game is it, though?"

"Crazy eights," said Nessa.

"Not blackjack?" asked Mrs. Kerr. "Or five-card stud?"

"What are those?" asked Jools.

"Some of the card games they play at the casino," said Mrs. Kerr.

"Are they hard?" asked Alix. "Can you teach us?"

Mrs. Kerr thought for a moment.

"No, not too hard," she said. "Yes, I suppose I could teach you."

She poured Goldfish crackers into four bowls and sat down at the table. Everyone had a bowl of Goldfish crackers. She taught them some card games where you had to put some of your crackers on the table every time you did certain things. Whoever won got to take all of those crackers. That was the "gambling" part.

Mrs. Kerr won every time. Her bowl filled up with crackers.

"Never gamble," she said. "You could lose all your Goldfish."

She took her bowl of Goldfish and her glass of water and went back into the living room.

They went back to playing crazy eights. The Goldfish were gone, but they found some pretzels and played the game of seeing who could whistle first after eating one.

They must have gotten noisy, because Mrs. Kerr said could they please do something quieter or go in the bedroom.

In the bedroom, Jools tried to teach Alix and Nessa a dance from her dance class, but the room was too small to do it right. They ended up just lying on their backs on the floor, laughing. The floor was hard, so they crawled up on one of the beds. And then the light bulb in the ceiling burned out. Jools reached to turn on the lamp over the bed, but Alix said, "No, let's let it be dark for a while! We can tell scary stories!"

They each tried to think of one.

Jools told a story from a book she had read, about two kids who are exploring in the woods when they come across some old abandoned houses. The houses are all falling apart and overgrown, like everyone left.

"PineyWild," said Alix.

"Shh," said Jools.

It was a ghost town. And then it turns out that two old people still live there.

"The old people are funny and jolly, though," said Jools, "so it wasn't *that* scary."

"I have a scary story," said Nessa. "One time when my cat, Nosey, was still a kitten, she climbed up in the tree by our house. I called and called, but she wouldn't come down. I could tell she was afraid, because she was yowling. So I climbed up to get her. It's a big pine tree with a lot of branches. It's easy to climb.

"She crawled right onto my shoulder, and I started to climb down. She was still yowling. I was holding onto her with one hand, but then she started to crawl down my back. I grabbed on with my other hand, kind of leaning against the tree trunk, and the branch I was standing on snapped. We both came crashing down.

"That was scary, but the scariest part was that on the way down, the skin on the top of my hand got ripped open by a jagged branch or something. When

I landed, at first I was just surprised. Noscy was surprised, too. She was standing there like, What just happened? Then I looked down at my hand, and the skin was flapped back. I could see the inside of it. That was the really scary part. Or maybe not so much scary, as creepy."

Alix shivered.

"Did you have to get stitches?" asked Jools.

"They glued it," said Nessa. "You can still see a scar, a little bit."

Alix couldn't think of a scary story. Also, it wasn't that dark anymore. Their eyes had adjusted. Light from the living room shone in under the door. It felt cozy.

"Listen," said Nessa. "You can hear my grandma snoring."

They listened. They could. That made it feel even cozier.

Tomorrow, Alix thought, or the next day, someone else would be in this room. What would it be like, she wondered, to have new neighbors every week?

"Do you make friends with everyone who stays here?" she asked. "Do you ever wish people would stay longer?"

"Sometimes I do," said Nessa. "I wish you guys would stay longer. That would be fun. Maybe you can come back next summer."

"I hope so," said Alix. "Then it could be like we're cousins who come to visit every year."

This made Jools think of when they talked about pretending Mrs. Kerr was their aunt. She told Nessa about how they were all going to faint when long-lost Uncle Dorian showed up while they were eating their spaghetti dinner.

Nessa laughed.

"I would definitely faint if my grandpa showed up," she said. "He died before I was even born."

"Was his name Dorian?" asked Alix.

"No," said Nessa. "His name was Arturo. When my grandma talks about him, she calls him Artie."

"Uncle Artie," said Alix. "And Aunt Lila."

"Uncle Cal," said Nessa. "And Aunt Viv."

"If we were actual cousins," said Jools, "it would be your mom and dad who were our aunt and uncle."

Jools. She was always so accurate. It was true, though.

"We didn't get to meet your mom," said Alix. "And we hardly met your dad."

"You can meet them next year," said Nessa.

This made it feel as if next year would really happen. Alix hoped that it would.

But right now was good, too. It was perfect. She went inside her thoughts for a minute to make a memory picture of how perfect it was.

Rose and Trevor were waiting there. They took her by surprise.

"What about us?" they said.

Maybe they weren't there. Maybe they didn't say that. Especially Trevor, since dogs can't talk. Maybe it was just Alix's imagination.

Just in case, she zapped a thought message out to them: *But you're having fun without me, too, right? And soon, we'll all be together again.*

Rose and Trevor looked at each other, then back at Alix. Trevor wagged his tail. Rose had an expression of *You're right, we are. And we will.* They waved, then they evaporated or something, and Alix was back in the cozy, not-really-that-dark room with Jools and Nessa.

Who were singing "Silent Night."

Alix didn't know why they were singing it, in the middle of summer, but it felt just right.

It felt perfect. Everything felt perfect.

She sang, too.

Back in Shembleton, Rose looked at Trevor curiously.

"Did you just say something?" she asked.

Trevor looked back as if to say, No—I thought it was you.

"Oh, never mind," said Rose.

chapter 8

GOING HOME

And then, just like that, vacation was over. The trunk was even more crammed than before they left home, though they didn't really have anything new.

Dad muttered as he tried to get the lid down.

"Let me try," said Mom. She jostled a few things around and squished in some sticking-up parts, then pushed down on the lid. It popped back open.

She jumped up and bounced on it with all of her weight. It rose again, like toast in a toaster. She jumped and bounced again. Finally, they heard the click. They all waited for it to spring back up, but it stayed shut.

"I think we got her," said Dad. "Let's roll."

Across the street, the little chunk of ocean glittered with sunlight.

"Good-bye, ocean," said Alix. "This was the best time I ever had."

"You always say that," said Jools.

"It's always true," said Alix.

"Couldn't we stay just one more day?" asked Jools.

"Nope," said their dad. "We're out of money. Or should I say clams?"

"Ha, ha, ha," said their mom.

A screen door fell shut above them. Nessa and Mrs. Kerr appeared at the upstairs porch railing, in their nightgowns.

"Bye, Alix!" Nessa called down softly. "Bye, Jools!"

"Bye-bye, Treffreys," said Mrs. Kerr. "Come again! Stay longer!"

"Thank you so much, Lila," said Mom. "We had a wonderful time."

"I'm so glad," said Mrs. Kerr.

Alix ran over and stood below the porch.

"Let's be friends forever," she said to Nessa. "Even if we never see each other again."

"Okay," said Nessa. "But come back next summer."

"I will," said Alix. "If I can talk my mom and dad into it."

"Let's go, Alix," called her mom.

"Bye!" said Alix, then ran and got into the car, too.

Nessa leaned on the railing and waved as the car backed out of the driveway.

"Is it dumb to make friends with people who are just going to leave?" she asked.

"I don't think it's ever a mistake to make a friend," said Mrs. Kerr. "But I'll bet your friend Charlotte would like to see you today."

"Can she come over?" asked Nessa. "Can we go pick her up?"

"Let's give her a call," said Mrs. Kerr. "In a little while, when people are awake."

The ocean winked at the Treffreys from between houses and motels.

When they got to the place with the roller coaster and the Ferris wheel and the mini golf, it was quiet, and mostly empty. Because it was morning.

"Can we go to this place next time?" said Jools. "Just for an hour or two?"

"There are lots of things still to do here," said Mom.

"I'd like to check out the shipwreck museum," said Dad. "If we come again."

This wasn't exactly a yes. But it wasn't exactly a no, either.

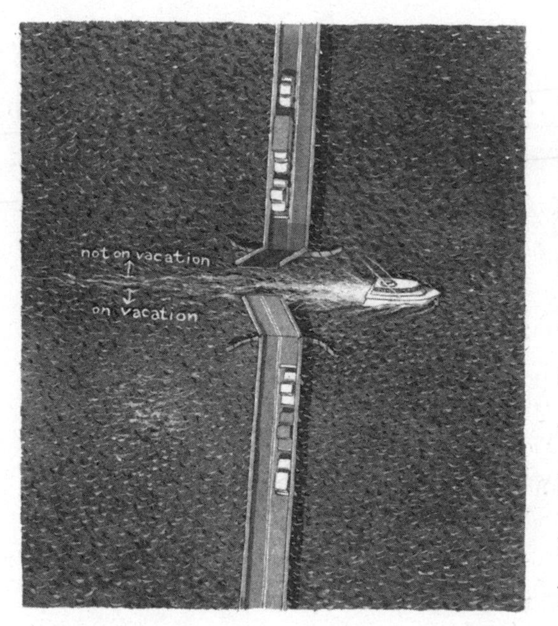

They drove out onto the road that went from the island to the mainland. This time the drawbridge was raised to let a boat pass through. The boat left a trail of ripples behind it. When the drawbridge lowered and the Treffreys drove across, Alix could still see the faint line of ripples. It was like a line between being on vacation and not being on vacation.

This time, Alix and Jools knew how long the drive

would be. They settled into it. Jools took out her book and started to read. Alix daydreamed. She let her favorite parts of the week float in and out of her thoughts. There were so many.

The first flat tire took them all by surprise. The sudden, quick thumping got louder and louder. They jolted and thumped off the highway, onto the side of the road, and stopped. Dad said a word that he almost never said, and that Alix and Jools were not allowed to say, ever. He said it three times.

"Cal," said Mom.

"Sorry," he said. "Don't worry, kids. It's just a flat tire."

Luckily, they had a spare tire in the trunk of the car. Underneath all their stuff.

"At least it's not raining," said Jools, as they piled everything up against the guardrail. It looked as if it might, though.

She and Alix watched their parents change the tire. It was so cool that they knew how. Alix felt proud of

them. Everyone who drove by could see that Cal and Viv Treffrey knew exactly what to do.

They all helped load up the trunk again, got back in the car, and drove on.

Jools opened her book. Mom was driving. Dad looked things up on his phone and fiddled around with the radio.

Alix sat cross-legged and looked out the window. All that was out there was hills and trees. A lot of trees. They looked just like the little sponge trees for model trains at the craft store. And then, down in a valley, she saw a real train, far enough away to look tiny. It was as if they were riding through a giant model-train display. Maybe she would make one someday, at least the landscape part. With one of the ponds that looks like real water, but when you touch it, it's hard. Or she could also make one that *was* real water. That might be even better. Maybe the trees should be real, too. Tiny real trees. And tiny real people. Ha-ha-ha, just kidding. She had seen a model-train display once, at a big greenhouse, that had the real trees and real water. Though not the real people.

And then the car started to vibrate and wobble. And to thump, again. Louder and louder, the thumping. Mom gripped the steering wheel, looking over her shoulder. She flicked on the emergency flashers and herded the wobbling, thumping, and blinking car once more off the road, onto the shoulder. They wobbled and thumped to a stop. And sat there in silence. Mom still gripped the steering wheel. She looked straight ahead. Then she drummed her fingers on the steering wheel, *ta-da-dum*, *ta-da-dum*, and turned to Dad.

"We don't have any more spare tires hidden away back there, do we?" she asked.

"Nope," he said. "I'm afraid not."

He took his phone out and started scrolling.

"Where are we?" he asked, as he put the phone to his ear.

"Just west of Exit 31," said Mom.

They didn't have to empty out the trunk this time, but they opened it to take out the cooler. And the jack and the crowbar. Dad jacked up the front of the car and took the bum tire off, so it would be ready to go when the new tire arrived.

Meanwhile, Mom and Jools and Alix spread the beach blanket on the hillside.

"We might as well have lunch," said Mom, "while we're waiting."

They had a couple of peanut-butter sandwiches, with no jelly, and cold, leathery pizza. Also, some spotty bananas and water bottles full of water. The potato chips, which had not been in the cooler, were warm and toasty, though kind of smashed.

"Bite sized!" said Alix.

"If you're an ant," said Dad, as he pulled a wad of potato chip crumbs out of the bag. They dribbled from between his fingers like confetti. He tilted back his head and dropped the crumbs into his mouth, then dusted off his hands and licked his fingers.

"Hunger is the best sauce!" said Alix.

No one said anything to that. They were too busy gnawing on the leathery pizza as traffic whizzed by.

The gray sky hung low.

The humidity was 1,000 percent.

When a tow truck pulled up behind their car, Dad went over to talk to the man who jumped out. The two of them carried the new tire from the truck to the car. Then Dad and Mom walked off, talking quietly. They stopped about thirty feet away.

Alix and Jools watched Dad pull out his wallet, thumb through the bills, and put it back in his pocket. Mom held her arms folded in front of her. They looked all serious.

"What do you think is happening?" asked Alix, between bites of mushy banana.

"I wonder if we don't have enough money," said Jools. "For the new tire."

But then their parents were laughing and walking back toward them. They were holding hands. So it must be okay.

"What were you guys talking about?" asked Alix.

"None of your beeswax, honeybee," said Dad.

He helped the tow-truck guy carry the old tire back to the truck, then counted out money from his wallet.

"Hey, Viv," he said. "Do you have a tenner?"

Mom got her purse from the car and walked over to Dad and the tire guy. Soon they were all saying "good-bye" and "thank you" and shaking hands. The tire guy got in his truck and drove away. He tooted his horn. The Treffreys all waved. Then they got in their car and drove away, too.

The third tire blew while they were going though one of the very long tunnels. There was no place to pull over. They had to keep going, with the *whump-whump-whump*ing all loud and ominous, and the emergency flashers flashing, as they slowed way, way down.

Dad said the swear word again, just once this time. Mom didn't tell him to stop. She just said, "Exactly."

She turned and smiled at Alix and Jools. It was an "oh, well" smile. A "what are you gonna do?" smile.

They limped out of the tunnel and onto the side of the road. Again. The cars and trucks that had been forced to go so slowly behind them whooshed forward.

There was no more picnic food. But there was a picnic table. Alix and Jools went over and sat on top of it. Dad sat on the passenger side, with the door open and his feet on the ground. He was making the phone call.

He pressed a finger against his non-phone ear to block out the noise.

Mom walked back and forth and in circles, her hands on her hips. She looked down at the ground, then up at the sky, then down at the ground again.

"Mom looks worried," said Alix.

"I brought the cards out," said Jools. "Let's play."

"Okay," said Alix. "Wanna play casino?"

"Sure," said Jools. She pulled the deck of cards from her shorts pocket and shuffled them.

"You are such a good shuffler," said Alix.

"Thanks," said Jools. "Blackjack or five-card stud?"

"Let's do blackjack," said Alix. "That's the one that has to add up to twenty-one, right?"

"Right," said Jools. She dealt the cards.

Alix studied her hand.

"Hit me!" she said.

"What are you playing?" asked Mom.

"It's called blackjack," said Alix.

"But just for fun," said Jools. "Not for Goldfish.

Because we don't have any, for one thing."

"Where did you learn to play blackjack?" asked Mom.

"From Mrs. Kerr," said Alix. "We used Goldfish instead of money. She won every time. She told us, 'Never gamble: you could lose all your Goldfish.'"

"So we're just playing for fun," said Jools, again.

Mom laughed.

"Mrs. Kerr is a wise woman," she said. "I wish she had been with us at the casino last night."

"Why?" asked Alix.

"We didn't lose all our Goldfish," said Mom. "But we lost a few more than we planned on. All these flat tires are killing us."

"Are we poor?" asked Alix.

Mom put her arms around both of them.

"We are rich in so many ways," she said.

"We aren't rich in tires," said Alix.

"We will be now," said Mom.

"Are we rich enough to get home?" asked Jools.

Mom laughed again.

"We'll get home," she said. "Don't worry."

Then she sat down and said, "Start over, and deal me in."

They kept expecting the fourth tire to blow, but it never did.

It was a kind of miracle.

They got home in the middle of the night. Boskey Street was as dark as when they had left it, as if no time had passed at all. Alix and Jools stumbled from the car to the house. Before they knew it, they were in their beds.

But changing into her nightgown had woken Alix up a little bit. She lay there and thought how nice it felt to be in her own bed. Then she thought of what would be even nicer.

"Jools," she said, softly.

"Mmnph," said Jools.

"Can I come over to your bed?" asked Alix.

"Urnmf," said Jools. "Kay."

Alix hopped over and slipped in next to her. Jools

was facing the wall, so Alix was the outside spoon. The back of Jools's neck still smelled like sunblock. A secret souvenir of their vacation.

It had been so different from how she thought it would be. The water wasn't turquoise. There weren't any palm trees. Of all the things that had happened, not one of them was something she expected. Seagulls eating potato chips. Holding a falcon. Eating periwinkles, which were snails. Making friends. Jools wanting to be like her, Alix, even if it was only for a minute.

You never knew what amazing thing would happen next, that was for sure. Alix wondered if that might be true in Shembleton, too. If it could be true in everyday life, when you weren't on vacation. She felt that it could.

She sent a thought message to Rose and Trevor: *We're back! I can't wait to see you tomorrow!*

She sent one to Nessa, too: *I'm so glad we're friends!*

To Jools, she whispered, "I'm glad we're sisters."

Jools snored lightly. Because they were sisters, Alix could tell this was sleep language for "Same here."

She snuggled closer. It was so cozy. Being home, after an adventure. She felt herself drifting, drifting off like a piece of fluff, into the drowsy darkness of sleep. So easy, so soft, so floaty and warm . . . drift, drift, drift . . .

And yet even while she drifted . . .

. . . she could hardly wait until tomorrow.

AUTHOR'S NOTE

I learned so much while writing this book.

Special thanks to Rebecca Lessard, the founder and director of Wings of Wonder, a raptor sanctuary and rehabilitation center that has rehabilitation and education as its primary mission.

While visiting her, I watched a convalescing bald eagle fly across an aviary. I watched a snowy owl spin its head around backward. A peregrine falcon sat on my gloved hand, eating food that I held between my thumb and my forefinger. I learned a lot, including that after about five minutes, the falcon starts to feel pretty heavy, and your arm gets tired.

For more information on Wings of Wonder, aka W.O.W., go to their website, wingsofwonder.org. I am so grateful to Rebecca for generously sharing her time and her expertise. There are a number of places like this around the country. Maybe there is one near you. Search for "raptor rehabilitation + [name of your state]."

Thanks also to Erwin "Duke" Elsner, past president of the Michigan Entomological Society (his list of accomplishments goes on and on), who advised me on June beetles. One of the things he said was, "They are clumsy fliers." I love when scientists say facts that sound, to me, like poetry. That line, slightly altered, found its way into this story.

One of the first rules an aspiring writer hears is Write What You Know. But it doesn't have to be something you've known forever. Learning new things is one of the best parts.

All my advisors did their best to inform me, and I

did my best to get it right. Still, any errors are mine.

P.S. There is one error I made on purpose. June beetles don't actually have eyes and eyebrows that express surprise in the same way ours do, but I drew them that way anyhow. I believe their eyes actually look more like this:

eyeball close-up

HOW TO MAKE A SEA-GLASS (OR STONE) NECKLACE

I have always liked making things, and learning how to make things. Alix Treffrey does, too. Do you?

Since Alix scraped the paper from a twist tie to get to the silvery wire inside, I tried it out to see if it would work. I wrapped it around a piece of sea glass. Then I tried using some wire I found in my junk drawer. It was longer than the twist tie, so it was easier to use. I twisted it with my fingers and figured out how to do it myself. So long as you leave a loop for the ribbon, it will work.

But now I have learned a few tips that make it work even better. Here they are:

THINGS YOU WILL NEED

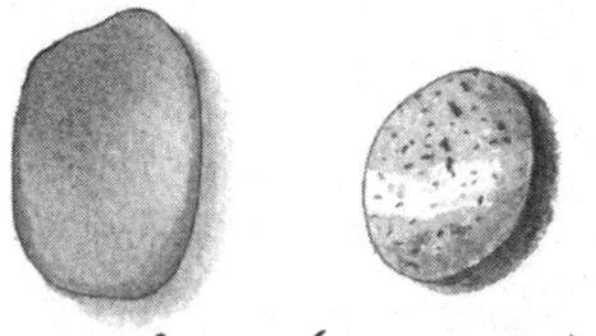

1. A piece of sea glass, or a stone that you like. (Not too big. Not a boulder!)

2. Wire: Eighteen inches of whatever wire you can find. I don't recommend scraping twist ties. Ask a grown-up if there is any wire in the house. Or use 20- or 24-gauge silver-plated wire from the craft store. It comes in small amounts, it's super-pretty, and it's not that expensive. At this writing, a package with 5 meters/16.4 feet of wire will make 11 necklaces at 64 ccnts apiece.

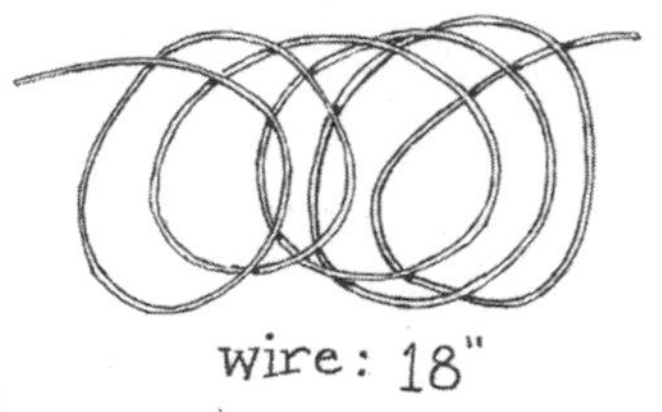

3. Needle-nose pliers: These are really helpful. Ask your grown-ups if you have pliers like these in the house. If not, you can use a pen or pencil, plus a pair of regular pliers, plus scissors.

this part can cut wire

needle-nose pliers

4. Ribbon: Or cord, or a necklace chain, or a piece of string. You'll need 30 inches.

5. Glasses: Safety glasses or regular glasses or goggles or even sunglasses. Something to protect your eyes when you cut the wire.

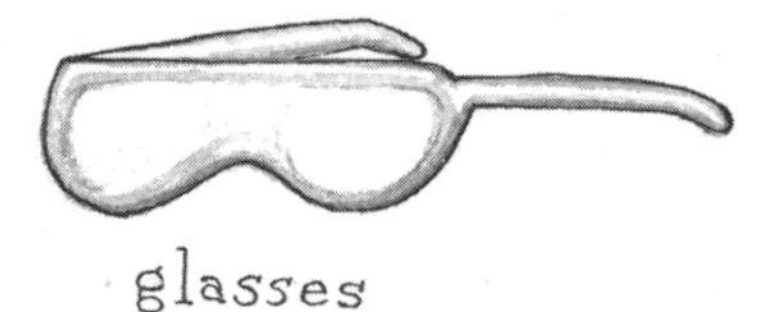

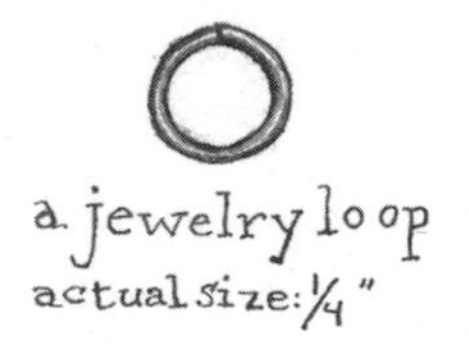

Optional: A jewelry loop. Adding this extra loop at the top helps the necklace to lie flat, but it's not necessary. You can find one at the craft store, or you can take one from an old necklace that no one wants anymore.

HOW TO MAKE THE NECKLACE

1. Bend the middle of your 18-inch piece of wire around the end of the needle-nose pliers (or a pen or pencil). *See pictures on page 232.*

2. Wrap it around one more time, and pull it snug.

3. Twist the two sides of the wire together, as tightly as you can. Keep twisting until the twist goes about halfway down

your piece of sea glass or stone.

4. Place your sea glass or stone on top of the wire, leaving about 1/8 inch of twist above the glass/stone. Wrap the two sides of the wire upward across the glass/stone in an X.

5. Wrap the wires up/across the back of the glass/stone to the "neck." Wrap them around the neck, in opposite directions (one clockwise, one the other way) a couple of times each. Do this as tightly as you can.

6. Clip the wires so they end in the front. This way, they won't scratch anyone, or catch on clothing. Squish them snug with your pliers.

7. Optional: Put a jewelry loop through the top loop. When you open it with your pliers, do it back-to-front (as if it were going to be a spiral), not to the sides, which will bend the metal. Squeeze it closed again with your pliers.

8. Slip your ribbon (or whatever) through the loop, and tie the two ends together in a knot. Make sure the necklace is big enough to go over someone's head.

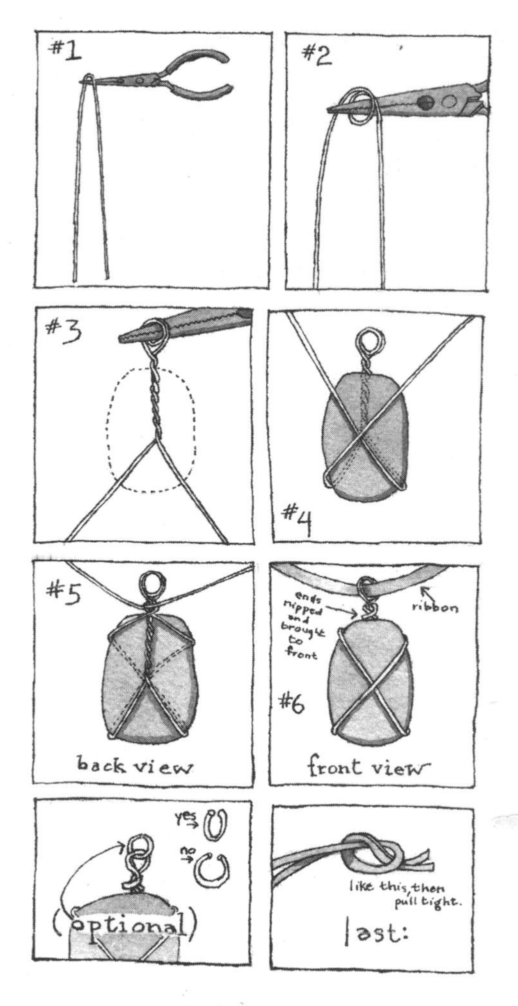

TA-DA! YOU DID IT!